Enid B

D0612426

The
Secret
Mountain

AWARD PUBLICATIONS LIMITED

For further information on Enid Blyton please visit *www.blyton.com*

Hardback ISBN 978-1-84135-750-8
Paperback ISBN 978-1-84135-676-1

Illustrated by Dudley Wynne
Cover illustration by Val Biro

First published 1941 by Basil Blackwell Limited
This edition first published 2009

Published by Award Publications Limited,
The Old Riding School, The Welbeck Estate,
Worksop, Nottinghamshire, S80 3LR

www.awardpublications.co.uk

Hardback 09 1
Paperback 13 4

Printed in the United Kingdom

Contents

The Beginning of the Adventures

One bright sunny morning, very early, four children stood on the rough grass of a big airfield, watching two men busily checking the engines of a gleaming white aeroplane.

The children looked rather forlorn, for they had come to say goodbye to their father and mother, who were to fly themselves to Africa.

'It's fun having a famous father and mother who do all kinds of marvellous flying feats,' said Mike. 'But it's not such fun when they go away to far-off countries!'

'Well, they'll soon be back,' said Nora, Mike's twin sister. 'It will only be a week till we see them again.'

'I somehow feel it will be longer than that,' said Mike gloomily.

'Oh, don't say things like that!' said Peggy. 'Make him stop, Jack!'

Jack laughed and slapped Mike on the shoulder. 'Cheer up!' he said. 'A week from today you'll be here again to welcome them back, and there will be cameramen and newspaper men crowding round to take your picture – son of the most famous air-pilots in the world!'

The children's father and mother came up, dressed in flying suits. They kissed and hugged the children.

'Now, don't worry about us,' said their mother. 'We

shall soon be back. You will be able to follow our flight
by reading what the newspapers say every day. We will
have a party when we come home, and you shall all stay
up till eleven o'clock!'

'Gracious!' said Jack. 'We shall have to start going to
bed early every night to get ready for such a late party!'

It was rather a feeble joke, but everyone was glad to
laugh at it. One more hug all round and the two flyers
climbed into the cockpit of their tiny aeroplane, whose
engines were now roaring in a most business-like way.

Captain Arnold was to pilot the aeroplane for the first
part of the flight. He waved to the children. They waved
back. The aeroplane engines took on a deeper, stronger
note, and the machine began to move gently over the
grass, bumping a little as it went.

Then, like a bird rising, the wheels left the ground
and the tiny white plane rose into the air. It circled
round twice, rose high, and then sped off south with a
drone of powerful engines. The great flight had begun!

'Well, I suppose the White Swallow will break another
record,' said Mike, watching the aeroplane become a
tiny speck in the blue sky. 'Come on, you others. Let's

go and have some lemonade and buns.'

Off they went and were soon sitting round a little table in the airfield's restaurant. They were so hungry that they ordered twelve buns.

'It's a bit of luck getting off from school for a couple of days like this,' said Mike. 'It's a pity we've got to go back today. It would have been fun to go to a cinema or something.'

'Our train goes from London in two hours' time,' said Peggy. 'When does yours go?'

'In three hours,' said Jack, munching his bun. 'We shall have to go soon. It will take us over an hour to get to London from here, and you girls don't want to miss your train.'

'We'll all look in the newspapers each day and see where Mummy and Daddy have got to,' said Peggy. 'And we'll look forward to meeting you boys here again in about a week's time, to welcome the plane back! Gosh, that *will* be exciting!'

'I still feel rather gloomy,' said Mike. 'I really have got a nasty feeling that we shan't see Dad and Mummy again for a long time.'

'You and your nasty feelings!' said Nora laughing. 'By the way, how's Prince Paul?'

Prince Paul was a boy at Mike's school. He and the children had had some strange adventures together the year before, when the Prince had been captured and taken from his land of Baronia to be kept prisoner in an old house that had once belonged to smugglers. The children had rescued him – and now Paul had been sent to the same school as his friends, Mike and Jack.

'Oh, Paul's all right,' said Mike. 'He was furious because the headmaster wouldn't allow him to come with Jack and me to see Dad and Mummy off.'

'Well, give him our love and tell him we'll look forward to seeing him in the holidays,' said Peggy, who was very fond of the little Prince.

'Come on – we really must go,' said Mike. 'Where's the taxi? Oh, there it is. Get in, you girls, and we'll be off. Jack and I will have time to come and see you safely into your train.'

Before evening came all four children were safely back at their two schools. Prince Paul was watching for his friends, and he rushed to meet Jack and Mike.

'Did you see them off?' he cried. 'Did you see the evening paper? There's a picture of Captain and Mrs Arnold in it.'

Sure enough the evening papers were full of the big flight that the famous pilots were making. The children read them proudly. It was fun to have such a famous father and mother.

'I'd rather have a pilot for a father than a king,' said Prince Paul enviously. 'Kings aren't much fun, really – but airmen are always doing marvellous things!'

For the next two days the papers were full of the plane's magnificent flight – and then a horrid thing happened. Mike ran to get the evening paper, and the first thing that met his eye was a great headline that said:

NO NEWS OF THE ARNOLDS.
STRANGE SILENCE. WHAT HAS HAPPENED
TO THE WHITE SWALLOW?

The White Swallow was the name given to the beautiful aeroplane flown by Captain and Mrs Arnold. Mike went pale as he read the headlines. He handed the paper to Jack without a word.

Jack glanced at it in dismay. 'What can have happened?' he said. 'I say – the girls will be awfully upset.'

'Didn't I tell you I felt gloomy when I saw Dad and Mummy off?' said Mike. 'I *knew* something was going to happen!'

The girls were just as upset as the boys. Nora cried and Peggy tried to comfort her.

'It's no good telling me they will be all right,' wept Nora. 'They must have come down in the middle of Africa somewhere, and goodness knows what might happen. They might be eaten by wild animals, or get lost in the forest or—'

'Nora, they've got food and guns,' said Peggy. 'And if the plane has had an accident, well, heaps of people will be looking and searching day and night. Let's not look on the dark side of things till we know a bit more.'

'I wish we could see the boys,' said Nora, drying her eyes. 'I'd like to know what they say.'

'Well, it's half-term holiday the week-end after next,' said Peggy. 'We shall see them then.'

To the children's great disappointment, there was no news of their parents the next day – nor the next day either. Then, as the days slipped by, and the papers forgot about the lost flyers, and printed other fresher news, the children became more and more worried.

Half-term came, and the four of them went to London, where they were to stay for three days at their parents' flat. Miss Dimity, an old friend of theirs, was to look after them for that short time. Prince Paul was to join them that evening. He had to go and see his own people first, in another part of London.

'What's being done about Dad and Mummy?' asked Mike, feeling glad to see Dimmy, whom they all loved.

'My dear, you mustn't worry – everything is being done that can possibly *be* done,' said Dimmy. 'Search parties have been sent out all over the district where it is thought that Captain and Mrs Arnold may have come down. They will soon be found.'

Dimmy took them all to a cinema, and for a while the children forgot their worries. Prince Paul joined them after tea, looking tremendously excited.

'I say, what do you think?' he cried. 'My father has sent me the most wonderful birthday present you can think of – guess what it is!'

'A pink elephant,' said Mike at once.

'A blue bed-jacket!' said Nora.

'A clockwork mouse!' said Peggy.

'A nice new rattle!' cried Jack.

'Don't be silly,' grinned Paul, who was now quite used to the English children's teasing ways. 'You're all wrong – he's given me an aeroplane of my very own!'

The four children stared at Paul in the greatest surprise. They knew that Paul's father was a rich king – but even so, an aeroplane seemed a very extravagant present to give to a small boy.

'An *aeroplane*!' said Mike. 'Gosh – if you aren't lucky, Paul! But you are too young to fly it. It won't be any use to you.'

'Yes, it will,' said Paul. 'My father has sent me his finest pilot with it. I can fly all over your little country of England and get to know it very well.'

A voice came up from the London street below. 'Paper! Evening paper! Lost aeroplane found! White Swallow found!'

With a yell the four children rushed down the stairs to buy a paper. But what a dreadful disappointment for them! It was true that the White Swallow had been found – but Captain and Mrs Arnold were not with it. They had completely disappeared!

The children read the news in silence. The aeroplane had been seen by one of the searching planes, which had landed nearby. Something had gone wrong with the White Swallow and Captain Arnold had plainly been putting it right – then something had happened to stop him.

'And now they've both disappeared, and, although all the people living round have been questioned about them, nobody knows anything – or they say they don't, which comes to the same thing,' said Peggy, almost in tears.

'I wish to goodness we could go out to Africa and look for them,' said Mike, who hadn't really much idea of how enormous a place Africa was.

Prince Paul slipped a hand through Mike's arm. His eyes shone.

'We *will* go!' he said. 'What about my new aeroplane! We can go in that – and Pilescu, my pilot, can take us! He is always ready for an adventure! Don't let's go back to school, Mike – let's go off in my aeroplane!'

The others stared at the little Prince in astonishment. What an idea!

'We couldn't possibly,' said Mike.

'Why not?' said Paul. 'Are you afraid? Well, I will go by myself then.'

'Indeed, you won't!' cried Jack. 'Mike – it's an idea! We've had marvellous adventures together – this will be another. Let's go – oh, do let's go!'

In the Middle of the Night

Not one of the five children thought of the great risk and danger of the adventure they were so light-heartedly planning.

'Shall we tell Dimmy?' said Nora.

'Of course not,' said Jack scornfully. 'You know what grown-ups are – why, Dimmy would at once telephone Paul's pilot and forbid him to take us anywhere.'

'Well, it seems horrid to leave her and not tell her anything,' said Nora, who was very fond of Miss Dimity.

'We'll leave a note for her that she can read when we are well away,' said Mike. 'But we really mustn't do anything to warn her or anyone else. My word – what a good thing that Paul had that aeroplane for his birthday!'

'When shall we go?' said Paul, his big dark eyes shining brightly. 'Now – this very minute?'

'Don't be an idiot, Paul,' said Jack. 'We've got to get a few things together. We ought to have maps, I think, for one thing.'

'I can't read maps,' said Nora. 'They look like squiggly puzzles to me.'

'They really aren't difficult,' said Jack. 'They'll help us find our way. But where can we get them – I'm sure I don't know.'

'Pilescu, my pilot, can get everything we want,' said Prince Paul. 'Don't worry.'

'But how will he know what to get?' asked Mike. 'I hardly know myself what we ought to take.'

'I will tell him he must find out,' said Paul. 'Show me where your telephone is Mike, and I will tell him everything.'

Soon Paul was holding a most extraordinary talk with his puzzled pilot. In the end Pilescu said he must come round to the flat and talk to his small master. He could not believe that he was really to do what Paul commanded.

'I say – suppose your pilot refuses to do what you tell him?' said Jack. 'I'm sure he will just laugh and tell us to go back to school and learn our tables or something!'

'Pilescu is my man,' said the little Prince, putting his small chin into the air, and looking very royal all of a sudden. 'He has sworn an oath to me to obey me all my life. He has to do what I say.'

'Suppose he tells your father?' said Mike.

'Then I will no longer have him as my man,' said Paul fiercely. 'And that will break his heart, for he loves me and honours me. I am his prince, and one day I will be his king.'

'You talk like a history book,' said Peggy with a laugh. 'All right, Paul – you try to get Pilescu to do what we have planned. He'll soon be here.'

In twenty minutes Pilescu arrived. He was a strange-looking person, very tall, very strong, with fierce black eyes and a flaming red beard that seemed on fire when it caught the sun.

He bowed to all the children in turn, for his manners were marvellous. Then he spoke to Paul in a curiously gentle voice.

'Little Prince, I cannot believe that you wish me to do what you said on the telephone. It is not possible. I cannot do it.'

Prince Paul flew into a rage, and stamped on the floor, his face bright red, and his dark eyes flashing in anger.

'Pilescu! How dare you talk to me like this? My father, the king, told me that you must do my smallest wish. I will not have you for my man. I will send you back to Baronia to my father and ask him for a better man.'

'Little Prince, I held you in my arms when you were born, and I promised then that you should be my lord,' said Pilescu, in a troubled voice. 'I shall never leave you, now that your father has sent me to be with you. But do not ask me to do what I think may bring danger to you.'

'Pilescu! Shall I, the king's son, think of danger!' cried the little Prince. 'These are my friends you see here. They are in trouble and I have promised to help them. Do you not remember how they saved me when I was kidnapped from my country of Baronia? Now it is my turn to help them. You will do what I say.'

The other four children watched in astonishment. They had not seen Paul acting the prince before. Before ten minutes had gone by the big Baronian had promised to do all that his haughty little master demanded. He bowed himself out and was gone from the flat before Dimmy came to find out who the visitor was.

'Good, Paul!' said Mike. 'Now all we've got to do is to

wait till Pilescu lets us know how he got on.'

Before the night was gone Pilescu telephoned to Prince Paul. The boy came running to the others, his face eager and shining.

'Pilescu has found out everything for us. He has bought all we need, but he says we must pack two bags with all we ourselves would like to have. So we must do that. We must leave the house at midnight, get into the car that will be waiting for us at the corner – and go to the airfield!'

'Gosh! How exciting!' said Mike. The girls rubbed their hands, thrilled to think of the adventure starting so soon. Only Jack looked a little doubtful. He was the eldest, and he wondered for the first time if they were wise to go on this new and strange adventure.

But the others would not even let him speak of his doubts. No – they had made up their minds, and everything was ready except for the packing of their two bags. They were going; they were going!

The bags were packed. The five children were so excited that they really did not know what to pack, and when the bags were full, not one child could possibly have said what was in them! With trembling hands they did up the leather straps, and then Mike wrote out a note for Dimmy.

He stuck the note into the mirror on the girls' dressing-table. It was quite a short note.

Dimmy Dear,

Don't worry about us. We've gone to look for Daddy and Mummy. We'll be back safe and sound before long.

Love from all of us

Dimmy had been out to see a friend and did not come back until nine o'clock. The children had decided to get into bed fully dressed, so that Dimmy would not have any chance of asking awkward questions.

Dimmy was rather surprised to find all the children so quiet and good in bed. They did not even sit up to talk to her when she came into the bedrooms to kiss them all goodnight. She did not guess that it was because they were not in their night clothes!

'Dear me, you must all be tired out!' she said in surprise. 'Well, goodnight, my dears, sleep well. You still have another day's holiday, so we will make the most of it tomorrow.'

All the children lay perfectly still until they heard Dimmy go into her bedroom and shut the door. They listened to her movements, and then they heard the click of her bedroom light being turned off.

'Don't get out of bed yet,' whispered Jack to Mike. 'Give Dimmy time to get to sleep.'

So for another half-hour or so the children lay quiet – and Nora fell asleep! Peggy had to wake her up, and the little girl was most astonished to find that she had to get up in the dark, and that she had on her day clothes! But she soon remembered what a big adventure was beginning, and she rubbed her eyes, and went to get a wet sponge to make her wider awake.

'What's the time?' whispered Mike. He flashed his torch on to the bedroom clock – half-past eleven. Nearly time to leave the house.

'Let's go to the dining-room and hunt round for a few biscuits first,' said Jack. 'I feel hungry. Now for goodness sake be quiet, everyone. Paul, don't trip over anything – and, Nora, take those squeaky shoes off! You sound like a dozen mice when you creep across the bedroom!'

So Nora took off her squeaky shoes and carried them. Jack and Mike took the bags, and the five children made their way quietly down the passage to the dining-room. They found the biscuit tin and began to munch. The noise of the biscuits being crunched in their teeth sounded very loud in the silence of the night.

'Do you think Dimmy will hear us munching?' said Nora anxiously. She swallowed her piece of biscuit too soon and a crumb caught in her throat. She went purple in the face, and tried hard not to cough. Then an enormous cough came, and the others rushed at her.

'Nora! Do be quiet!' whispered Jack fiercely. He caught the cloth off the table and wrapped it round poor Nora's head. Her coughs were smothered in it, but the little girl was very angry with Jack.

She tore off the cloth and glared at the grinning boy. 'Jack! You nearly smothered me! You're a horrid mean thing.'

'Sh!' said Mike. 'This isn't the time to quarrel. Listen – the clock is striking twelve.'

Dimmy was peacefully asleep in her bedroom when the five children crept to the front door of the flat. They opened it and closed it very quietly. Then down the stone stairway they went to the street entrance, where another big door had to be quietly opened.

'This door makes an awful noise when it is closed,' said Mike anxiously. 'You have to bang it. It will wake

everyone!'

'Well, don't shut it then, silly,' said Jack. 'Leave it open. No one will bother about it.'

So they left the big door open and went down the street, hoping that they would not meet any policemen. They felt sure that a policeman would think it very strange for five children to be out at that time of night!

Luckily they met no one at all. They went down to the end of the street, and Mike caught Jack's arm.

'Look – there's a car over there – do you suppose it is waiting for us?'

'Yes – that's our car,' said Jack. 'Isn't it, Paul?'

Paul nodded, and they crossed the road to where a big blue and silver car stood waiting, its engine turned off. The children could see the blue and silver in the light of a street lamp. Paul's aeroplane was blue and silver too, as were all the royal aeroplanes of Baronia.

A man slipped out of the car and opened the door silently for the children. His uniform was of blue and silver too, and, like most Baronians, he was enormous. He bowed low to Paul.

Soon the great car was speeding through the night. It went very fast, eating up the miles easily. The children were all tremendously excited. For one thing it was a great thrill to be going off in an aeroplane – and who knew what exciting adventures lay in store for them!

They came to the airfield. It was in darkness, except for lights in the middle of the field, where the beautiful aeroplane belonging to Prince Paul stood ready to start.

'I am to take you right up to the aeroplane in the

car,' said the driver to Prince Paul, who sat in front with him.

'Good,' said Paul. 'Then we can all slip into it, and we shall be off before anyone really knows we are here!'

An Exciting Journey

The big blue and silver car drove silently over the bumpy field until it came to the aeroplane. Pilescu was there, his red beard shining in the light of a lamp. With him was another man just as big.

'Hello, Ranni!' said Prince Paul joyfully. 'Are you coming too? I'm so glad to see you!'

Ranni lifted the small Prince off the ground and swung him into the air. His broad face shone with delight.

'My little lord!' he said. 'Yes – I come with you and Pilescu. I think it is not right that you should do this – but the lords of Baronia were always mad!'

Paul laughed. It was easy to see that he loved big Ranni, and was glad that the Baronian was coming too.

'Will my aeroplane take seven?' he asked, looking at it.

'Easily,' said Pilescu. 'But now, come quickly before the mechanics come to see what is happening.'

They all climbed up the little ladder to the cockpit. The aeroplane inside was like a big and comfortable room. It was marvellous. Mike and the others cried out in amazement.

'This is a wonderful aeroplane,' said Mike. 'It's much better than even the White Swallow.'

'Baronia has the most marvellous planes in the world,' said Pilescu proudly. 'It is only a small country, but our inventors are the best.'

The children settled down into comfortable armchair seats. Paul, who was tremendously excited, showed everyone how the seats unfolded, when a spring was touched, and became small beds, cosy and soft.

'Gosh!' said Jack, making his seat turn into a bed at once, and then changing it back to an armchair, and then into a bed again. 'This is like magic. I could do this all night!'

'You must settle down into your seats quickly,' ordered Pilescu, climbing into the pilot's seat, with big Ranni just beside him. 'We must be off. We have many hundreds of miles to fly before the sun is high.'

The children settled down again, Paul chattering nineteen to the dozen! Nobody felt sleepy. It was far too exciting a night to think of sleep.

Pilescu made sure the children had all fastened their seat belts, and started the engines, which made a loud and comfortable noise. Then, with a slight jerk, the aeroplane began to run over the dark field.

It bumped a little – and then, like a big bird, it rose into the air and skimmed over the long line of trees that stood at the far end of the big field. The children hardly knew that it had left the ground.

'Are we still running over the field?' asked Mike, trying to see out of the window near him.

'No, of course not,' said Ranni laughing. 'We are miles away from the airfield already!'

'Goodness!' said Peggy, half-startled to think of the enormous speed at which the plane was flying. The children had to raise their voices when they spoke, because the engines of the plane, although specially muffled, still made a great noise.

That flight through the dark night was very strange to the children. As soon as the plane left the ground its wheels rose into its body and disappeared. They would descend again when the aeroplane landed. It flew through the darkness as straight as an arrow, with Pilescu piloting it, his eyes on all the various things that told him everything he needed to know about the plane.

'Why did Ranni come?' Prince Paul shouted to Pilescu.

'Because Ranni can take a turn at piloting the plane,' answered Pilescu. 'Also there must be someone to look after such a crowd of children!'

'We don't need looking after!' cried Mike indignantly. 'We can easily look after ourselves! Why, once when we ran away to a secret island, we looked after ourselves for months and months!'

'Yes – I heard that wonderful story,' said Pilescu. 'But I must have another man with me, and Ranni was the one I could most trust. We may be very glad of his help.'

No one knew then how glad they were going to be that big Ranni had come with them – but even so, Ranni was very comforting even in the plane, for he brought the children hot cocoa when they felt cold, and produced cups of hot tomato soup which they thought tasted better than any soup they had ever had before!

'Isn't it exciting to be drinking soup high up in an aeroplane In the middle of the night?' said Peggy. 'And I do like these biscuits. Ranni, I'm very glad you came with us!'

Big Ranni grinned. He was like a great bear, yet as gentle as could be. He adored little Paul, and gave him far too much to eat and drink. They all had bars of nut chocolate after the soup, and Pilescu munched as well.

The plane had been flying very steadily indeed – in fact, the children hardly noticed the movement at all – but suddenly there came a curious jerk, and the plane dropped a little. It happened two or three times, and Paul didn't like it.

'What's it doing?' he cried.

Mike laughed. He had been up in aeroplanes before, and he knew what was happening at that moment.

'We are only bumping into air-pockets,' he shouted to Paul. 'When we get into one we drop a bit – so it feels as if the plane is bumping along. Wait till we get into a big air-pocket – you'll feel funny, young Paul!'

Sure enough, the plane slipped into a very big air-pocket, and down it dropped sharply. Paul nearly fell off his big armchair, and he turned quite green.

'I feel sick,' he said. Ranni promptly presented him with a strong paper bag.

'What's this for?' asked Paul, in a weak voice, looking greener than ever. 'There's nothing in the bag.'

The other four children shouted with laughter. They felt sorry for Paul, but he really did look comical, peering into the paper bag to see if there was anything there.

'It's for you to be sick in, if you want to be,' shouted Jack. 'Didn't you know that?'

But the paper bag wasn't needed after all, because the plane climbed high, away from the bumpy air-pockets, and Paul felt better. 'I shan't eat so much chocolate

25

another time,' he said cheerfully.

'I bet you will!' said Jack, who knew that Paul could eat more chocolate than any other boy he had ever met. 'I say – isn't this a gorgeous adventure? I hope we see the sun rise!'

But they didn't, because they were all fast asleep! Nora and Peggy began to yawn at two o'clock in the morning, and Ranni saw them.

'You will all go to sleep now,' he said. He got up and helped the two girls to turn their big armchairs into comfortable, soft beds. He gave them each a pillow and a very cosy warm rug.

'We don't want to go to sleep,' said Nora in dismay. 'I shan't close my eyes. I know I shan't.'

'Don't then,' said Ranni with a grin. He pulled the rugs closely over the children and went back to his seat beside Pilescu.

Nora and Peggy and Paul found that their eyes closed themselves – they simply wouldn't keep open. In three seconds they were all sound asleep. The other two boys did not take much longer, excited though they were. Ranni nudged the pilot and Pilescu's dark eyes twinkled as he looked round at the quiet children.

He and Ranni talked in their own language, as the plane roared through the night. They had travelled hundreds of miles before daylight came. It was marvellous to see the sun rising when dawn came.

The sky became full of a soft light that seemed alive. The light grew and and changed colour. Both pilots watched in silence. It was a sight they had often seen and were never tired of.

Golden light filled the aeroplane when the sun showed a golden rim over the far horizon. Ranni switched off the electric lights at once. The world lay below, very beautiful in the dawn.

'Blue and gold,' said Ranni to Pilescu, in his own language. 'It is a pity the children are not awake to see it.'

'Don't wake them, Ranni,' said Pilescu. 'We may have a harder time in front of us than they know. I am hoping that we shall turn and go back, once the children realise that we cannot possibly find their parents. We shall not stay in Africa very long!'

The children slept on. When they awoke it was about eight o'clock. The sun was high, and below the plane was a billowing mass of snowy whiteness, intensely blue in the shadows.

'Is it snow?' said Paul, rubbing his eyes in amazement. 'Pilescu, I asked you to fly to Africa, not to the North Pole!'

'It's fields and fields of clouds,' said Nora, looking with delight on the magnificent sight below them. 'We are right above the clouds. Peggy, look – they seem almost solid enough to walk on!'

'Better not try it!' said Mike. 'Ranni, you might have woken us up when dawn came. Now we've missed it. I say, I am hungry!'

Ranni became very busy at the back of the plane, where there was a proper little kitchen. Soon the smell of frying bacon and eggs, toast and coffee stole into the cabin. The children sniffed eagerly, looking down at the fields of cloud all the time, marvelling at their

27

amazing beauty.

Then there came a break in the clouds and the five children gave shouts of joy.

'Look! We are over a desert or something. Isn't it weird?'

The smooth-looking desert gave way to mountains, and then to plains again. It was most exciting to watch.

'Where are we?' asked Mike.

'Over Africa,' said Ranni, serving bacon and eggs to everyone, and putting hot coffee into the cups. 'Now eat well, for it is a long time to lunch-time!'

It was a gorgeous meal, and most exciting. To think that they had their supper in London – and were having their breakfast over Africa! Marvellous!

'Do you know whereabouts our parents came down,

Pilescu?' asked Mike.

'Ranni will show you on the map,' said the pilot. 'Soon we must go down to get more fuel. We are running short. You children are to stay hidden in the plane when we land on the airfield, for I do not want to be arrested for flying away with you!'

'We'll hide all right!' said Paul, excited. 'Where is that map, Ranni? Let us see it. Oh, how I wish I had done better at geography. I don't seem to know anything about Africa at all.'

Ranni unfolded a big map, and showed the children where Captain and Mrs Arnold's plane had been found. He showed them exactly where their own plane was too.

'Goodness! It doesn't look very far from here to where

the White Swallow was found!' cried Paul, running his finger over the map.

Ranni laughed. 'Further than you think,' he said. 'Now look – we are nearing an airfield and must get fuel. Go to the back of the plane and hide under the pile of rugs there.'

So, whilst the plane circled lower to land, the five children snuggled under the rugs and luggage. They did hope they wouldn't be found. It would be too dreadful to be sent back to London after coming so far.

In a Very Strange Country

A number of men came running to meet the plane as it landed beautifully on the runway. Pilescu climbed out of the cockpit and left Ranni on guard inside. The children were all as quiet as mice.

The blue and silver plane was so magnificent that all the groundsmen ran round it, exclaiming. They had never seen such a beauty before. Two of them wanted to climb inside and examine it, but Ranni stood solidly at the entrance, his big body blocking the way. Pilescu spoke to the mechanics and soon the plane was taking in an enormous amount of fuel.

'Pooh! Doesn't it smell horrid?' whispered Paul. 'I think I'm going to choke.'

'Don't you dare even to sneeze,' ordered Jack at once, his voice very low but very fierce.

So Paul swallowed his choking fit and went purple in the face. The girls couldn't bear the smell either, but they buried their faces deeper in the rug and said nothing.

A man's voice floated up to the cockpit, speaking in broken English.

'You have how many passengers, please?' he asked.

'You see me and my companion here,' answered Pilescu shortly.

The man seemed satisfied, and walked round the

31

plane admiring it. Pilescu took no notice of him, but began to look carefully into the engines of the plane. He noticed something was wrong and shouted to Ranni.

'Come down here a minute and give me a hand.' Ranni stepped down the ladder and went to stand beside Pilescu. As quick as lightning one of the airfield men skipped up the ladder to the cockpit and peered inside the plane.

It so happened that Mike was peeping out to see if all was clear at that moment. He saw the man before the man saw him, and covered his face again, nudging the others to keep perfectly still.

Ranni saw that the man had gone up to the cockpit and he shouted to him. 'Come down! No one is allowed inside our plane without permission.'

'Then you must give me permission,' said the man, whose quick eye had seen the enormous pile of rugs at the back, and who wished to examine it. 'We have had news that five children are missing from London, and there is a big reward offered from the King of Baronia if they are found.'

Pilescu muttered something under his breath and ran to where the mechanics had just finished refuelling the plane. He pushed them away and made sure nobody was still nearby. Ranni went up the steps in a flash, and tipped the inquisitive man down them. Pilescu leapt into the plane and slipped into the pilot's seat like a fish sliding into water.

There was a good deal of shouting and calling, but Pilescu ignored it. He started the plane and it ran swiftly over the ground. With a crowd of angry men rushing after it, the plane taxied to the end of the field and then rose gently into the air. Pilescu gave a short laugh.

'Now it will be known everywhere that we have the children on board. Get them out, Ranni. They were very good and they must be half smothered under those rugs.'

The five children were already crawling out, excited to think of their narrow escape.

'Would we have been sent back to London?' cried Paul.

'I peeped out but the man didn't see me!' shouted Mike.

'Are we safe?' said Peggy, sitting down in her comfortable armchair seat again. 'They won't send up planes to chase us, will they?'

'It wouldn't be any use,' said Ranni, with a grin. 'This is the fastest plane on the airfield. No – don't worry. You are all right now. But we must try to find the place where the White Swallow came down, for we do not want to land on any more airfields at the moment.'

The day went on, and the children found it very thrilling to look out of the windows and see the mountains, rivers, valleys and plains slipping away below them. They longed to go down and explore them. It was wonderful to be over a strange land, and see it spread out below like a great map.

Towards the late afternoon, as the children were eating sweet biscuits and chocolate, and drinking lemonade, which by some miracle Ranni had iced, Pilescu gave a shout.

Ranni and he put their heads together over the map, and the two men spoke excitedly in their own language. Paul listened, his eyes gleaming.

'What are they saying?' cried Mike impatiently. 'Tell us, Paul.'

'They say that we are getting near the place where the White Swallow came down,' said Paul. 'Ranni says he had been in this part of the country before. He was sent to get animals for our Baronian Zoo, and he knows the people. He says they live in tiny villages, far from any towns and they keep to themselves so that few others know them.'

The plane flew more slowly and went down lower. Ranni searched the ground below them carefully as the plane flew round in big circles.

But it was Mike who first saw what they were all eagerly looking for! He gave such a shout that the girls nearly fell off their seats, and Ranni turned round with a jump, half-expecting to see one of the children falling out of the plane!

'Ranni! Look – there's the White Swallow! Oh, look – oh, we've passed it! Pilescu, Pilescu go back! I tell you I saw the White Swallow!'

The boy was so excited that he shook big Ranni hard by the shoulder, and would have done the same to the pilot except that he had been warned not to touch Pilescu when he was flying the machine. Ranni looked back, and gave directions to Pilescu.

In a moment the plane circled back and was soon over the exact place where the gleaming white plane stood still and silent. The children gazed at it. To think that they were looking at the very same plane they had waved goodbye to some weeks before – but this time the two famous pilots were not there to wave back.

'I can't land very near to it,' said Pilescu. 'I don't know how Captain Arnold managed to land there without crashing. He must be a very clever pilot.'

'He is,' said Peggy proudly. 'He is one of the best in the world.'

'I shall land on that smooth-looking bit of ground over there,' said Pilescu, flying the plane lower. 'We may bump a bit, children, because there are rocks there. Get ready for a jolt!'

The plane flew even lower. Then Pilescu found that

he could not land with safety, and he rose into the air again. He circled round once more and then went down. This time he let down the wheels of the plane and they touched the ground. One ran over a rock and the plane tilted sideways. For one moment everyone thought that it was going over, and Pilescu turned pale. He did not want to crash in the middle of an unknown country!

But the plane was marvellously built and balanced and it righted itself. All the children had been thrown roughly about in their seats, and everything in the cabin had slid to one side.

But the five children soon sorted themselves out, too excited even to look for bruises. They rushed to the door of the cockpit, each eager to be out first. Ranni shouted to them.

'Stay where you are. I must go out first to see what there is to be seen.'

Pilescu stopped the engines, and the big throbbing noise died away. It seemed strange to the children when it stopped. Everything was so quiet, and their voices seemed suddenly loud. It took them a little time to stop shouting at one another, for they always had to raise their voices when they were flying.

Ranni got out of the cockpit, his gun handy. No one appeared to be in sight. They had landed on rough ground, strewn with boulders, and it was really a miracle that they had landed so well. To the left, about two miles away, a range of mountains rose. To the right was a plain, dotted with trees that the children did not know. Small hills lay in the other directions.

'Everything looks very strange, doesn't it?' said Mike.

'Look at those funny red-brown daisies over there. And even the grass is different!'

'So are the birds,' said Peggy, watching a brilliant red and yellow bird chasing a large fly. A green and orange bird flew round the plane, and a flock of bright blue birds passed overhead. They were not a bit like any of the birds that the children knew so well at home.

'Can we get out, Ranni?' called Mike, who was simply longing to explore. Ranni nodded. He could see no one about at all. The five children rushed out of the plane and jumped to the ground. It was lovely to feel it beneath their feet again.

'I feel as if the ground ought to bump and sway like the plane,' said Nora, with a giggle. 'You know – like when we get out of a boat.'

'Well, I jolly well hope it doesn't,' said Jack. 'I don't want an earthquake just at present.'

The sun was very hot. Pilescu got out some sun-hats for the five children and for himself and Ranni too. They had a sort of veil hanging down from the back to protect their spines from the sun. None of them were wearing very many clothes, but even so they felt very hot.

'I'm jolly thirsty,' said Mike, mopping his head. 'Let's have a drink, Ranni.'

They all drank lemonade, sitting in the shade of the plane. The sun was now getting low, and Pilescu looked at the time.

'There's nothing more we can do today,' he said. 'Tomorrow we will find some local people and see what we can get out of them by questioning them. Ranni thinks he can make them understand, for he picked up some of their language when he was here hunting animals for the Baronian Zoo.'

'Well, surely we haven't got to go to bed already?' asked Nora in dismay. 'Aren't we going to explore a bit?'

'There won't be time – the sun is setting already,' said Ranni. As he spoke the sun disappeared over the horizon, and darkness fell around almost at once. The children were surprised.

'Day went into night, and there was no evening,' said Nora, looking round. 'The stars are out, look! Oh, Mike – Jack – aren't they enormous?'

So they were. They seemed far bigger and brighter than at home. The children sat and looked at them, feeling almost afraid of their strange beauty.

Then Nora yawned. It was such an enormous yawn that it set everyone else yawning too, even big Ranni! Pilescu laughed.

'You had little sleep last night,' he said. 'You must have plenty tonight. In this country we must get up very early whilst it is still cool, for we shall have to rest in the shade when the sun climbs high. So you had better go to sleep very soon after Ranni has given you supper.'

'Need we sleep inside the plane?' said Jack. 'It's so hot there. Can we sleep out here in the cool?'

'Yes,' said Ranni. 'We will bring out rugs to lie on. Pilescu and I will take it in turns to keep watch.'

'What will you watch for?' asked Peggy, in surprise. 'Not enemies, surely?'

'Well, Captain and Mrs Arnold disappeared just here, didn't they?' said Pilescu solemnly. 'I don't want to wake up in the morning and find that we have disappeared too. I should just hate to go and look for myself!'

Everyone laughed – but the children felt a little nervous too. Yes – this wasn't nice, safe old England. This was a strange, unknown country, where strange, unexpected things might happen. They moved a little closer to red-bearded Pilescu. He suddenly seemed very safe and protective as he sat there in the starlight, as firm and solid as one of the big dark rocks around!

Waiting for News

Ranni provided a good meal, and Pilescu built a camp-fire, whose red glow was very comforting. 'Wild animals will keep at a safe distance if we keep the fire going well,' said Pilescu, putting a pile of brushwood nearby. 'Ranni or I will be keeping guard tonight, and we will have a fine fire going.'

Rugs were spread around the fire, whose crackling made a very cheerful sound. The five children lay down, happy and excited. They had come to the right place – and now they were going to look for Captain and Mrs Arnold. Adventures lay behind them, and even more exciting ones lay in front.

'I shall never go to sleep,' said Nora, sitting up. 'Never! What is that funny sound I hear, Ranni?'

'Baboons in the hills,' said Ranni. 'Never mind them. They won't come near us.'

'And now what's *that* noise?' asked Peggy.

'Only a night-bird calling,' said Ranni. 'It will go on all night long, so you will have to get used to it. Lie down, Nora. If you are not asleep in two minutes I shall put you into the plane to sleep there by yourself.'

This was such a terrible threat that Nora lay down at once. It was a marvellous night. The little girl lay on her back looking up at the enormous, brilliant stars that hung like bright lamps in the velvet sky. All around her she heard strange bird and animal sounds. She was warm and comfortable and the fire at her feet crackled most comfortingly. She took a last look at big Ranni, who sat with his back to the plane, gun in hand, and then shut her eyes.

'The children are all asleep,' said big Ranni to Pilescu in his own language. 'I think we should not have brought them on this adventure, Pilescu. We do not know what will happen. And how shall we find Captain and Mrs Arnold in this strange country? It is like seeking for a nut on an apple tree!'

Pilescu grunted. He was very tired, for he had flown the plane all the way, without letting Ranni help. Ranni was to watch three-quarters of the night, and Pilescu was to sleep – then he would take the rest of the watch.

'We will see what tomorrow brings,' he said, his big red beard spreading over his chest as his head fell forward in sleep. And then another noise was added to the other night-sounds – for Pilescu snored.

He had a wonderful snore that rose and fell with his breathing. Ranni was afraid that he would wake up the children and he nudged him.

But Pilescu did not wake. He was too tired to stir. Jack awoke when he heard the new sound and sat up in alarm. He listened in amazement.

'Ranni! Ranni! Some animal is snorting round our camp!' he called. 'Are you awake? Can't you hear him?'

Ranni smothered an enormous laugh. 'Lie down, Jack,' he said. 'It is only our good friend Pilescu. Maybe he snores like that to keep wild animals away. Even a lion might run from that noise!'

Jack grinned and lay down again. Good gracious, Pilescu made a noise as loud as the aeroplane! Well – almost, thought Jack, floating away into sleep again.

Ranni kept watch most of the night. He saw shadowy shapes not far off, and knew them to be some kind of night-hunting animals. He watched the stars move down the sky. He smelt the fragrance of the wood burning on the fire, and sometimes he reached out his hand and threw some more into the heart of the leaping flames.

A little before dawn Ranni awoke Pilescu. The big Baronian yawned loudly and opened his eyes. At once he knew where he was. He spoke to Ranni, and then went for a short walk round the camp to stretch his legs and get wide awake.

Then Ranni slept in his turn, his hand still on his gun. Pilescu watched the dawn come, and saw the whole country turn into silver and gold. When daylight was fully there he awoke everyone, for in such a hot country they must be astir early whilst the air was still cool.

The children were wild with excitement when they awoke and saw their strange surroundings. They ran round the camp, yelling and shouting, whilst Ranni cooked a delicious-smelling meal over the camp fire.

'Hey, look! Here's a kind of little lake!' shouted Jack. 'Let's wash in it. Ranni, Pilescu! Could we bathe in this lake, do you think?'

'Not unless you want to be eaten by crocodiles,' said Ranni.

Nora gave a scream and tore back to the camp at top speed. Ranni grinned. He went to look at the lake. It was not much more than a pond, really.

'This is all right,' he said. 'There are no crocodiles here. All the same, you mustn't bathe in it, for there may be slug-like things called leeches, which will fasten on to your legs and hurt you. Please remember to be very careful indeed in this strange country. Animals that you only see at the Zoo in England run wild here all over the place.'

This was rather an alarming idea to the two girls. They did a very hasty wash indeed, but the three boys splashed vigorously. The air was cool and delicious, and every one of the children felt as if they could run for miles. But they only ran to the camp beside the plane, for they were so hungry, and breakfast smelt so good. The hot coffee sent its smell out, and the frying bacon sizzled and crackled in the pan.

'What's the plan for today, Pilescu?' asked Jack. 'Do we find someone and ask if they know anything of the White Swallow and its pilots?'

'We are in such a remote part of Africa, that the people round here might never have seen a plane before. But Ranni is going to the nearest village to try and get news,' said Pilescu, ladling out hot bacon on to the plates.

'But how does he know where the next village is?' asked Mike in wonder, looking round. 'I can't see a thing.'

'You haven't used your eyes,' said Ranni, with a smile. 'Look over there.'

The children looked in the direction to which he was pointing, where low hills lay. And they all saw at once what Ranni meant.

'A spire of smoke!' said Mike. 'Yes – that means a fire

– and fire means people. So that's where you are going, Ranni? Be careful, won't you?'

'My gun and I will look after one another,' said big Ranni with a grin, and he tapped his pocket. 'I shall not be back till nightfall, so be good whilst I am gone!'

Ranni set off soon after breakfast, carrying food with him. He wore his sun-hat, for the sun was now getting hot. The children watched him go.

'I do wish we could have gone with him,' said Jack longingly. 'I hope he will have some news when he comes back.'

'Come, you children can wash these dishes in water from the pool,' called Pilescu. 'Soon it will be too hot to do anything. Before it is, we must also find some firewood ready for tonight.'

Pilescu kept the children busy until the sun rose higher. Then when its rays beat down like fire, he made them get into the shade of the plane. Paul did not want to, for he enjoyed the heat, but Pilescu ordered him to go with the others.

'Pilescu, it is not for you to order me,' said the little Prince, sticking his chin into the air.

'Little Paul, I am in command now,' said the big Baronian, gently but sternly. 'You are my lord, but I am your captain in this adventure. Do as I say.'

'Paul, don't be an idiot, or I'll come and get you into the shade by the scruff of your neck,' called Mike. 'If you get sunstroke, you'll be ill and will have to be flown back to London at once.'

Paul trotted into the shade like a lamb. He lay down by the others. Soon they were so thirsty that Pilescu

found himself continually getting in and out of the plane with supplies of cool lemonade from the little refrigerator there.

The children slept in the midday heat. Pilescu was sleepy too, but he kept guard on the little company, wondering how big Ranni was getting on. When the sun began to slip down the coppery sky, he mopped his brow and awoke the children.

'There is some tinned fruit in the plane,' he told Nora. 'Get it, and open the tins. It will be delicious to eat whilst we wait for the day to cool.'

Ranni did not come back until the sun had set with the same suddenness as the day before. The children watched and waited impatiently for him, and lighted the bonfire early to guide him.

Pilescu was not worried, for he knew that, although the spire of smoke had looked fairly near, it was really far away – and he knew also that Ranni would not be able to walk far when the midday heat fell on the land like flames from a furnace.

The little company sat round the fire, and above them hung the big bright stars. They all watched for Ranni to return.

'I do wonder if he will have any news,' said Nora impatiently. 'Oh, Ranni, do hurry! I simply can't wait!'

But she had to wait and so did everyone else. It was late before they heard the big Baronian shouting loudly to them. They all leapt up and trained their eyes to see him.

'There he is!' shouted Jack, who had eyes like a cat's in the dark. 'Look – see that moving shadow among those rocks?'

The shadow gave a shout and everyone yelled back in delight.

'Ranni! Hurrah! He's back!'

'What news, Ranni?'

'Hurry, Ranni, do hurry!'

The big Baronian came up to the fire. He was tired and hot. He dropped down to the rugs and wiped his hot forehead. Pilescu gave him a jug of lemonade and he drank it all in one gulp.

'Have you news, Ranni?' asked Pilescu.

'Yes – I have. And strange news it is too,' said Ranni. 'Give me some more sandwiches or biscuits, Pilescu, and I will tell my tale. Are you all safe and well?'

'Perfectly,' said Pilescu. 'Now speak, Ranni. What is this strange news you bring?'

Big Ranni Tells a Strange Tale

Ranni lighted his pipe and puffed at it. Everyone waited for him to begin, wondering what he had to tell them.

'I found a small camp,' said Ranni. 'Not more than four or five men were there. They had been out hunting. When they saw me coming they all hid behind the rocks in terror.'

'But why were they so afraid?' asked Nora in wonder.

'Well, I soon found out,' said Ranni. 'I can speak their language a little, because I have hunted round about this country before, as you know. It seems that they thought I was one of the strange folk from the Secret Mountain.'

'From the Secret Mountain!' cried Mike. 'What do you mean? What secret mountain?'

'Be patient and listen,' said Pilescu, who was listening closely. 'Go on, Ranni.'

'Somewhere not far from here is a strange mountain,' said Ranni. 'It is called the Secret Mountain because for years a secret and strange tribe of people have made their home in the centre of it. They are not like the people round about at all.'

'What are they like, then?' asked Jack.

'As far as I can make out their skins are a pale creamy-yellow, and their beards and hair are red, like Pilescu's and mine. They are thin and tall, and their eyes are green. No one belonging to any other tribe is allowed to mix with them, and no one has ever found out the entrance into the Secret Mountain.'

'Ranni! This is a most wonderful story!' cried Prince Paul, his eyes shining with excitement. 'Is it really true? Oh, do let's go and find the secret mountain at once, this very minute!'

'Don't be an idiot, Paul,' said Mike, giving him a push. The little Prince was very excitable, and Mike and Jack often had to stop him when he wanted to rush off at once and do something. 'Be quiet and listen to Ranni.'

'All the people that live anywhere near are afraid of the Folk of the Secret Mountain,' said Ranni. 'They think that they are very fierce, and they do not come this way if they can possibly help it. When they saw me, with my red hair, they really thought I was a man from the Secret Mountain, and they were too terrified even to run away.'

'Did you ask them if they knew anything about Daddy and Mummy?' asked Peggy eagerly.

'Of course,' said Ranni. 'They knew nothing – but tomorrow a man is coming to our camp here, who saw the White Swallow come down, and who may be able to tell us something. But I think, children, that there is no doubt that Captain and Mrs Arnold were captured by the Folk of the Secret Mountain. We don't know why – but I am sure they are there.'

'We cannot search for them, then,' said Pilescu. 'We

must fly to the nearest town and bring a proper search party back here.'

'No, no, Pilescu,' cried everyone in dismay.

'*We* are going to look for our parents,' said Mike proudly. 'Pilescu, this is the third great adventure we children have had, and I tell you we are all plucky and daring. We will *not* fly away and leave others to follow this adventure.'

All the children vowed and declared that they would not go with Ranni and Pilescu, and the two men looked at one another over the camp fire.

'They are like a litter of tiger-cubs,' said Ranni in his own language to Pilescu.

Prince Paul laughed excitedly. He knew that Ranni wanted to follow the adventure himself, and that this meant that Paul too would be with him, for he would not leave his little master now. Paul turned to the other children.

'It's all right,' he said. 'We shan't go! Ranni means to help us.'

For a long time that night the little camp talked over Ranni's strange tale. Where was the Secret Mountain? Who were the strange red-haired people who lived there? Why had they captured Captain and Mrs Arnold? How in the world were the searchers to find the way into the mountain if not even the people round about know it? For a long time all these questions were discussed again and again.

Then Pilescu looked at his watch. 'It is very late!' he exclaimed. 'Children, you must sleep. Ranni, I will keep watch tonight, for you must be very tired.'

'Very well,' said Ranni. 'You shall take the first half of the night and I will take the other. We can do nothing but wait until tomorrow, when the man who saw the White Swallow will come to talk to us.'

Very soon all the camp was asleep, except Pilescu, who sat with his gun in hand, watching the moving animal shapes that prowled some distance away, afraid to come nearer because of the fire. Pilescu loved an adventure as much as anyone, and he thought deeply about the Folk of the Secret Mountain, with their creamy-yellow skins, red hair and curious green eyes.

The big Baronian was brave and fierce, as were all the men from the far-off land of Baronia, where Paul's father was king. He was afraid of nothing. The only thing he did not like was taking the five children into danger – but, as Ranni had said, they were like tiger-cubs, fierce and daring, and had already been through some astonishing adventures by themselves.

Morning came, and with it came the man who had seen the White Swallow come down. He was very tall, but with a sly and rather cruel face. Carrying three spears for him came a small, thin boy, with a sharp face and such a merry twinkle in his eyes that all the children liked him at once.

'Who is that boy?' asked Jack, curiously. Ranni asked the man, and he replied, making a scornful face.

'It's his nephew,' said Ranni. 'He is the naughty boy of the family, and is always running away, exploring the country by himself. Children of this tribe are not allowed to do this – they have to go with the hunters and be properly trained. This little chap is disobedient and wild, so his uncle has taken him in hand, as you see.'

'I like the look of the boy,' said Jack. 'But I don't like the uncle at all. Ask him about the White Swallow, Ranni. See if he knows anything about Captain and Mrs Arnold.'

Ranni did not speak the man's language very well, but he could understand it better. The man spoke a lot, waving his arms about, and almost acting the whole thing so that the children could nearly understand his story without understanding his words.

'He says he was hunting not far from here, keeping a good look-out for any of the Secret Mountain Folk, when he heard the sky making a strange noise,' said Ranni. 'He looked up, and saw a great white bird that said, "R-r-r-r-r-r-r," as loudly as a thunderstorm.'

The children shouted with laughter at this funny description of an aeroplane. Ranni could not help grinning, even though he knew the man had probably never seen a plane before, and went on with his translation.

'He says the big white bird flew lower, and came down over there. He stayed behind his tree without moving. He thought the big white bird would see him and eat him.'

Again everyone laughed. The tribesman grinned too, showing two rows of flashing white teeth. The little boy behind joined in the laughter, but stopped very suddenly when his uncle turned round and hit him hard on the side of the head.

'Oh my goodness!' shouted Jack in surprise. 'Why

shouldn't he laugh too?'

'Children of this tribe must not laugh if their elders
are present,' said Ranni. 'This man's nephew must often
get into serious trouble, I should think! He looks as if
he is on the point of giggling every minute!'

The man went on with his story. He told how he had
seen two people climb out of the big white bird, which
amazed him very much. Then he saw something that
frightened him even more than seeing the aeroplane
and the pilots. He saw some of the Folk of the Secret
Mountain, with their flaming red hair and pale skins!

He had been so interested in the aeroplane that he
had stayed watching behind his tree – but the sight of
the Secret Mountain Folk had given him such a scare
that his legs had come to life and he had run back
towards his village.

'So you didn't see what happened to the White Bird
people?' asked Ranni, deeply disappointed. The man
shook his head. The small boy watching, imitated him
so perfectly that all the children laughed, disappointed
though they were.

The man looked behind to see what everyone was
smiling at and caught his nephew making faces. He
strode over to him and knocked him down flat on the
ground. The boy gave a yell, sat up and rubbed his head.

'What a horrid fellow this man is,' said Pilescu in
disgust. 'Ranni, ask him if he can tell us the way to the
Secret Mountain.'

Ranni asked him. The man showed signs of fear as
he answered.

'He says yes, he knows the way to the mountain, but

he does not know the way inside,' said Ranni.

'Ask him if he will take us there,' said Pilescu. 'Tell him we will pay him well if he does.'

At first the man shook his head firmly when Ranni asked him. But when Pilescu took a mirror from the cabin of the plane, and showed the man himself in it, making signs to him that he would give it to him as well, the man was tempted.

'He thinks the mirror is wonderful. He is in the mirror as well as outside it,' translated Ranni with a grin. 'He says it would be a good thing to have it, because then if he is hurt or wounded, it will not matter – the man inside the mirror, which is himself too, will be all right, and he will be him instead.'

Everyone smiled to hear this. The man had never seen a mirror before, he had only caught sight of himself in pools. It seemed as if another himself was in the strange gleaming thing that the red-haired man was offering him. He stood in front of the mirror, making awful faces, and laughing.

Ranni asked him again if he would show them the way to the Secret Mountain if he gave him the mirror. The man nodded. The mirror was too much for him. Why, he had never seen anything like it before.

'Tell him we will start tomorrow at dawn,' said Pilescu 'I want to make sure that we have everything we need before we set off. Also I want to look at the engines of the White Swallow and our own plane to see that they are all ready to take off, should we find Captain and Mrs Arnold, and want to leave in a hurry!'

The children were in a great state of excitement.

They hardly knew how to keep still that day, even when the great heat came down, and they had to lie in the shade, panting and thirsty. It was so exciting to think that they really were to set off the next morning to the strange Secret Mountain.

'I'm jolly glad Ranni and Pilescu are coming with us,' said Nora. 'I do love adventures – but I can't help feeling a little bit funny in the middle of me when I think of those strange folk that live in the middle of a forgotten mountain.'

The Coming of Mafumu

Pilescu and Ranni tinkered about with the White Swallow, which stood not very far off, and with their own plane most of the day. The children, of course, had thoroughly examined the White Swallow, feeling very sad to think that Captain and Mrs Arnold had had to leave it so mysteriously.

Mike had thought that there might have been a note left to tell what had happened, but the children had found nothing at all.

'That's not to be wondered at,' said Pilescu. 'If they had had time to write a note, they would have had time also to fly off in the plane! As far as I can see there is nothing wrong with the White Swallow at all – though I can see where some small thing has been cleverly mended. It seems to me that Captain and Mrs Arnold were taken by surprise and had not time to do anything at all.'

'Both planes are fit to fly off at a moment's notice,' said Ranni, appearing beside Pilescu, very oily and black, his red hair hanging wet and lank over his forehead.

'Ought we to leave anyone on guard?' asked Mike. 'Suppose we come back and find that the planes have been damaged?'

Ranni frowned. 'We will lock them of course, but I

don't think anyone would damage them. I just hope a herd of elephants doesn't come and trample through them! We must just leave the planes and hope for the best.'

Pilescu had got ready big packages of food and a few warm clothes and rugs. Paul laughed when he saw the woollen jerseys.

'Good gracious, Pilescu, what are we taking those things for? I'd like to go about in a little pair of shorts and nothing else, like that small boy wears!'

'If we go into the mountains it will be much cooler,' said Pilescu. 'You may be glad of jerseys then.'

The day passed slowly by. The children thought it would never end.

'Why is it that time always goes so slowly when you are looking forward to something lovely in the future?' grumbled Mike. 'Honestly, this day seems like a week.'

But it passed at last, and the sudden night-time came. Monkeys chattered somewhere around, and big frogs in the washing-pool set up their usual tremendous croaking.

Next day, at dawn, their guide arrived, and behind him, as usual, came the little boy, his nephew, wearing his scanty shorts. The boy wore no hat at all, and the five children wondered why in the world he didn't get sunstroke.

'I suppose he's coming too,' said Jack, pleased. 'I wonder what his name is. Ask him, Ranni.'

The boy grinned and showed all his white teeth when Ranni shouted to him. He answered in a shrill voice:

'Mafumu, Mafumu!'

'His name is Mafumu,' said Ranni. 'All right, Mafumu, don't shout your name at us any more!'

Mafumu was so overjoyed at being spoken to by the big Ranni that he kept shouting and wouldn't stop.

'Mafumu, Mafumu, Mafumu!'

He was stopped in the usual way by his uncle, who slapped him hard on the head. Mafumu fell over, made a face at his uncle's back, and got up again. The children were very glad he was coming with them. They really couldn't help liking the cheeky little boy, with his twinkling black eyes and his flashing smile.

Ranni closed and locked the entrance door of the cockpit. Then, with a few backward glances at the two gleaming planes, the little company set off on their new adventure. They were silent as they left the camp, for all of them were wondering what might happen in the near future.

Then Mafumu broke the silence by lifting up his shrill voice and singing a strange slow song.

'Sounds a bit like one of the hymns we have in church,' said Mike. 'Oh no – his uncle is going for him again. How I wish he'd stop – he is always hitting poor Mafumu.'

Mafumu was slapped into silence. He came behind the whole company, sulking, carrying a simply enormous load. His uncle also carried a great many packages, balanced most marvellously on his head. Ranni explained that these people were used to carrying goods this way and thought nothing of taking heavy loads for many, many miles.

Soon the open space where the planes had landed

was left behind. The little company came towards what looked like a wood, but which was really a small forest that reached almost to the foot of the nearest mountain.

It was very dark in the forest after the glare of the sunlight. The trees were so thick, and heavy rope-like creepers hung down from them everywhere. The children could see no path at all to follow, but the tribesman led them steadily on, never once upsetting any of the many packages piled up on his head.

The chattering of monkeys was everywhere. The children saw the little brown creatures peering down at them, and laughed with delight to see a mother monkey holding a tiny baby in her arms. Other wild creatures scuttled away, and once their guide gave a loud shout and flung his spear at a large snake that slid silently away.

'Oooh,' said Nora, startled. 'I forgot there might be snakes here. I hope I don't tread on one. I say, isn't this an exciting forest? It's like one in a fairy-tale. I feel as if witches and fairies might come out at any moment.'

'Well, just make sure you don't wander off looking for fairy castles,' said Pilescu. 'There are probably lots of snakes and insects in the undergrowth, and you can be sure our guide is taking us by the safest path.'

Mafumu was enjoying himself. He was a long way behind his uncle, for the guide led the way, and Mafumu came at the tail of the company. Next to him was Jack, and Mafumu was doing his best to make friends with him.

He picked a brilliant scarlet blossom from one of the

trees and tried to stick it behind Jack's ear. Jack was most annoyed, and the others laughed till they cried at the sight of Jack with a red flower behind his ear. Mafumu thought that Jack didn't like the colour of the flower, so he picked a bright blue one and tried that.

Jack found himself decorated with this flower, and he took it from his ear crossly, whilst the others giggled again.

'Shut up, Mafumu,' he said.

Mafumu was very quick at picking up what he heard the children say, even though he did not understand the words. 'Shutup, shutup, shutup,' he repeated in delight. He called to Ranni. 'Shutup, shutup, shutup!'

Nobody could help laughing at Mafumu. He was so silly, so cheerful, so quick, and even when his uncle was unkind to him he was smiling a moment later.

He still badly wanted to make friends with Jack, and the next present he made to the boy was a large and juicy-looking fruit of some sort. He pressed it into Jack's hand, flashing his white teeth, and saying something that sounded like 'Ammakeepa-lotti-loo.'

Jack looked at the fruit. He smelt it. It had a most delicious scent, and smelt as sweet as honey. 'Is it safe to eat this, Ranni?' he called.

Ranni looked round and nodded. 'Yes – that is a rare fruit, only found in forests like these. Did Mafumu find it for you?'

'Yes,' said Jack. 'He keeps on giving me things. I wish he wouldn't.'

'Well, tell him to give them to me instead,' cried Peggy. 'I'd love to have those beautiful flowers and that delicious-looking yellow fruit. It looks like a mixture of an extra-large pear and a giant grape!'

Jack tasted it. It was the loveliest fruit he had ever had, so sweet that it seemed to be made of honey. The boy gave a taste to the two girls. They made faces of delight, and Nora called to Mafumu.

'Find some more please, Mafumu; find some more!'

'Shutup, shutup, shutup,' replied Mafumu cheerfully, quite understanding what Nora meant, and thinking that his answer was correct. He disappeared into the forest and was gone such a long time that the children began to be alarmed.

'Ranni! Do you think Mafumu is all right?' shouted Jack from the back of the line. 'He's been gone for ages. He won't get lost, will he?'

Ranni spoke to the guide in front. The man laughed and made some sort of quick answer.

'He says that Mafumu knows his forest as an ant knows its own anthill,' translated Ranni. 'He says, too, that he would not care at all if Mafumu were eaten by a crocodile or caught by a leopard. He doesn't seem at all fond of his small nephew, does he?'

'I think he's a horrid man,' said Peggy. 'My goodness – are there leopards about?'

'Well, you needn't worry even if there are,' said Ranni. 'Pilescu and I have guns, and our leader has plenty of spears ready.'

It was cool and dark in the forest and the little company were able to go for a long way without resting, twisting and turning through the trees. Frogs croaked somewhere, and birds called harshly. Jack spotted some brightly-coloured parrots, and there were some rather odd squirrel-like creatures that hopped from branch to branch. The monkeys were most interested in the

children, and a little crowd of them swung through the trees, following the company for quite a long way.

At last the forest came to an end. The trees became fewer, and the sun shone between, making golden freckles on the ground that danced and moved as the trees waved their branches.

'Well, that couldn't have been a very big forest if it only took us such a short time to go through,' said Mike.

'It is really a very big one,' said Pilescu. 'But we have only gone through a corner of it. If we went deeper into it we should not be able to get along. We should have to take axes and knives to cut our way through.'

The children were still worried about Mafumu, but he suddenly appeared again, bent nearly double under his old load and carrying a new load of the juicy-looking yellow fruit. He gave some to each child, grinning cheerfully.

'Oh, thanks awfully,' said Mike. 'This is just what I wanted – I *was* thirsty! This fruit melts in my mouth. Thanks awfully, Mafumu.'

'Thanksawfully, shutup,' said the little boy in delight.

'I think we'll all have a rest here,' said Pilescu. 'The sun is still high in the sky and we can't walk any further for it will be too hot once we are out of the forest. We will go on again when the sun is lower.'

Nobody felt very hungry, for they were all so hot. Mafumu found some other kind of fruit for everybody, not nearly so nice, but still, very juicy and sweet. His uncle ate no fruit, but took something from a pouch and chewed that.

All the children fell asleep in the noonday sun except Mafumu. He squatted down beside Jack and watched the boy closely. Jack grinned at him and even when he slept Mafumu stayed by his side.

The grown-ups sat talking quietly together. Ranni looked round at the sleeping company. 'The children have done well today,' he said to Pilescu. 'They must have a good night's rest tonight as well, for tomorrow we must climb high.'

'I wish that this adventure was over, and not just beginning,' said Pilescu uneasily, fanning Paul's hot face with a spray of leaves. The boy was so sound asleep that he felt nothing.

But not one of the children wished that the adventure was over. No – to be in the middle of one was the most exciting thing in the world!

A Very Long March

For two whole days the company marched valiantly onwards. The children were all good walkers except Paul, and as Ranni carried him on his shoulders when he was very tired, that helped a good deal.

They had now come to the mountains and the guide was leading them steadily upwards. It was tiring to climb always, but the children soon got used to it. Mafumu did not seem to mind anything. He skipped along, and went just as fast uphill as down. He had picked up some more words now, and used them often, much to the children's amusement.

'Goodgracious, shutup, hello, thanksawfully,' he would chant as he skipped along, his load of packages balanced marvellously and never falling. 'Hurryup, hurryup, hello!'

'Isn't he an idiot?' said Jack. But although the children laughed at his antics, they all liked the cheerful boy enormously. He brought them curious things to eat – toadstools that were marvellous when cooked – strange leaves that tasted of peppermint and were good to chew – fruit of all kinds, some sweet, some bitter, some too strange-tasting to eat, though Mafumu ate everything, and smacked his lips and rubbed his round tummy in delight.

On the second day, when the children were all climbing steadily, Mafumu saw a clump of bushes high up some way in front of them. They were hung with brilliant blue berries, which Mafumu knew were sweet and juicy. He took a short cut away from the path, and climbed to the bushes.

He stripped them of the blue berries and began to jump back to join the company. But on the way his foot caught against a loose stone that rattled down the hillside and fell against his uncle's leg.

In a fury the guide sprang at his nephew and caught hold of him. He beat him hard with his spear, and the little boy cried out in pain, trying his best to wriggle away.

'Oh, stop him, stop him!' yelled Jack, who hated unkindness of any sort. 'Mafumu was only getting berries for us. Stop, stop!'

But the guide did not stop, and Jack ran up to him. He wrenched the spear out of the man's hand and threw it down the hillside in anger, his face red with rage.

The spear went clattering down and was lost. The guide turned on Jack, but Ranni was beside him, talking sternly. The man listened, his eyes flashing. He said nothing, but turned to lead the way up the mountainside once more.

'What did you say to him, Ranni?' asked Mike.

'I told him he would not get paid if he hit anyone again,' said Ranni shortly. 'He was just about to strike Jack. Don't interfere again, Jack. I'll do the interfering.'

'Sorry,' said Jack, though he was still boiling with rage. Mafumu had got up from the ground, his face and arms covered with bruises. He ran to Jack and hugged him, speaking excitedly in his own language.

'Stop it, for goodness sake, Mafumu,' said Jack uncomfortably. 'Oh gosh, I wish you wouldn't. Do let go, Mafumu!'

'He says he will be your friend for ever,' said Ranni with a grin. 'He says he will leave his uncle and his tribe and come and be with the wonderful boy all his life. He says you are a king of boys!'

'King Jack, the king of boys!' shouted Mike, clapping Jack on the shoulder.

'Shut up,' growled Jack.

'Shutup, shutup, shutup,' echoed Mafumu happily, letting go of Jack and walking as close to his hero as he possibly could.

After that, of course, Mafumu adored Jack even more than before, and Jack got used to seeing the little boy always at his heels, like a shadow. He could not get rid of him, so he put up with it, secretly rather proud that Mafumu should have picked him out to be his friend.

It got steadily cooler as they all climbed higher. The mountains seemed never-ending.

'We shall never, never get to the top,' said poor Peggy, who had started a blister on one heel.

'We're not going to the top,' said Mike. 'All we are doing is climbing to a place where we can pass between two mountains. Ranni says we shall strike off to the east there, by that enormous rock, and make our way to a place where this mountain and the next one meet. There is a pass between them – and from there we can see the Secret Mountain!'

'Gosh!' said Paul. 'Are we as near as all that?'

'Well – not awfully near,' said Mike. 'But we'll get there sooner or later. Have you rubbed that stuff that Ranni gave you, all over your heel, Peggy?'

'Yes,' said Peggy. 'And I've put a wad of cotton-wool over the blister too. I shall be all right.'

'Well done,' said Mike. 'I don't think things like blisters ought to creep into adventures like ours!'

Everyone laughed. They had put on woollen jerseys now and were glad of them, especially when clouds rolled down the mountainside and covered them in mist. They were glad of hot drinks, too, heated over a fire of sticks.

Mafumu always knew where water was, and he brought it to the fire in the saucepan that Ranni gave him. It was easy to make hot cocoa with plenty of sugar in it from one of the packages, and how good it tasted!

They slept in a cave that night, stretched out on the rugs. The girls cuddled together for it was very cold. Mafumu slept on nothing at all, and did not seem to feel the cold in the least. He really was a tough little boy.

Ranni and Pilescu did not both sleep at the same time, but took turns at keeping watch – not only for any mountain leopard that might come into the cave, but also for any of the Folk from the Secret Mountain! They did not know what such strange people might do.

Mafumu was curled up on the rocky ground by Jack. Jack had offered him a share of the rug, but the boy would not take any of Jack's coverings. He even tried to cover Jack up, much to the amusement of everyone else.

'He wants to be your nurse,' chuckled Mike.

'Oh, do stop making jokes like that,' grumbled poor Jack. 'I can't help Mafumu behaving like this, can I? He will keep on doing it.'

'Tomorrow we shall see the Secret Mountain,' said Nora sleepily. 'I'm just longing to get my first glimpse of it. I wonder what it will be like.'

'I wonder if Mafumu's unpleasant uncle can possibly tell us any way to get into it,' said Mike. 'It's not going to be much good gazing at a secret mountain, if we don't know the secret of getting into the middle of it!'

'Do you suppose there are halls and rooms and passages in it?' said Peggy, cuddling closer to Nora to try and get warm. 'How I do love secret things!'

Mafumu took hold of Jack's rug and pulled it more closely over the elder boy and for once in a way Jack did not stop him. The boy was almost asleep. He lay there in the cave, his eyes closing.

'Goodnight, Mafumu,' said Jack sleepily.

'Hello, goodnight,' answered Mafumu, happy to be with his new friends.

'Tomorrow we shall see the – the – Secret – Mountain,' murmured Jack, and then fell fast asleep.

Tomorrow – yes, tomorrow!

The Secret Mountain

The next day dawned very misty. White clouds rolled round about the mountain pass, and it was difficult to see very far ahead. The children were most disappointed.

But as they walked steadily upwards towards the rocky pass between the two mountains, the sun began to shine more strongly through the mists, and soon the last fragments disappeared.

'Isn't everything glorious!' cried Mike, looking round. Below them lay the great hillside they had climbed, and in the distance, stretching for miles, they could see the rolling country of Africa. Above them towered the mountains and overhead was the blazing sky.

'All the colours look so much brighter here,' said Peggy, picking a brilliant orange flower and sticking it into her hat. 'Oh, Mafumu, for goodness sake!'

Mafumu had darted forward when he saw Peggy picking the flower, and had plucked a great armful of the orange flowers, which he now presented to her. The little girl laughed and took them. She didn't know what to do with them, but in the end she and Nora stuck them all round their hats.

'I feel like a walking garden now,' said Nora. 'I wish Mafumu wouldn't be so generous!'

'Soon we shall arrive at the place from which we get

our first glimpse of the Secret Mountain,' said Ranni.

That made everyone walk forward even more eagerly. For three hours they climbed towards the rocky pass, the guide leading the way, finding a path even when it seemed almost impossible to get by. Sometimes there was hard climbing to be done, and Ranni and Pilescu had to pull and push the children to get them up the hillside or over big rocks. Sometimes they passed through thick little copses of strange trees, where brilliant birds called to one another. It was all unknown country and most exciting.

At last they reached the top of the pass. From here they could see the other side of the range of mountains. Truly it was a marvellous place to stand! From this mountain peep-hole the little company could see both east and west – rolling country behind them for miles, disappearing into purple hills – and in front another range of mountains towering high into the sky, with a narrow valley in between the mountains they were on, and the range opposite.

Everyone stood silent, even the guide. It was surely the most wonderful sight in the world, the children thought. Then Paul spoke eagerly.

'Which is the Secret Mountain? Where is it? Quick, tell us!'

Ranni spoke to the guide, and he raised his spear and pointed with it. He spoke shortly to Ranni.

Ranni turned to the listening children. 'Do you see that mountain over there, with clouds rolling round it? Wait till they clear a little, and you will see that the mountain has a curiously flat top. You will also see that it has a yellowish look, because, so this fellow says, a rare yellow bush grows there, which at some season of the year turns a fiery red.'

This all sounded rather weird. The children gazed across to the opposite mountains – and each saw the one that had clouds covering it. As they watched, the clouds uncurled themselves, and became thinner and thinner, at last disappearing altogether. And then everyone could see the curious Secret Mountain!

It stood out boldly from the others because of its yellow appearance, and also because of its strange summit. This was almost flat, like a table-top. The guide raised his spear again, and pointed, muttering something to Ranni.

'He says that he has heard that the Folk of the Mountain sometimes appear on the top of it, and that they worship the sun from there,' said Ranni. 'Though how anyone could see people so far away I can't imagine. However, it is quite possible that there is a way up inside the mountain to the top.'

'Isn't it strange to think of a tribe of people taking such a strange home, and living there apart from everyone else?' said Jack in wonder.

'Oh, that has often happened,' said Pilescu. 'Sometimes there are tribes living apart from others in the middle of dense forests – sometimes on islands – sometimes even in deserts. But a mountain certainly seems one of the strangest places to choose.'

'I suppose they come out to hunt, and that is how the other people know about them,' said Mike.

'I think you are right,' said Ranni. 'Well – there's

the wonderful Secret Mountain – and here we are. The mountain won't come to us, so we must go to the mountain. Shall we set off again, Pilescu?'

The guide spoke rapidly to Ranni, making faces and waving his arms about.

'He says he doesn't want to come any further,' said Ranni. 'Is it any good his coming? He swears he doesn't know any way into the mountain.'

'He's going to come with us all the way,' said Pilescu firmly. 'He may find that he knows the way in after all, once we get there! Anyway, he won't get paid if he doesn't come.'

'Where *is* the money?' asked Nora. 'It's not being carried along with us, is it?'

'Of course not,' said Ranni with a laugh.

'Well, did you put it back into the cabin of the plane?' said Jack. 'You locked that.'

'No. I wrapped up the money carefully and hid it under the low branches of that big tree by the washing-pool before we left,' said Ranni. 'I shall tell our guide where it is when he has done his job – but not before!'

'That's a clever idea,' said Peggy. Ranni turned to the man and spoke to him again. He shook his head violently. Ranni shrugged his shoulders, and bade the little company set off.

They made their way along a rocky path, leaving the guide and Mafumu behind. But they had not gone very far before loud shouts came from the tribesman, and the children saw him leaping along to catch them up. Mafumu trotted behind, his face was one big smile.

His uncle spoke with Ranni, but Ranni shook his

head. The children could quite well guess what was happening – the man was asking to be paid, and Ranni was being determined. In the end the guide agreed to go with them once more, and Ranni promised to tell him where the money was as soon as they reached the Secret Mountain.

It was a good thing that their guide went with them, for the way he led them was one which they would never have found for themselves. It was a hidden way, so that the little company would not be seen by any watchers on the Secret Mountain.

Ranni and Pilescu had had no idea that there was this hidden path to the mountain. They would have tried to lead the party across the valley, over marshy ground, or through such thickly growing bushes that it would have been almost impossible to make their way through.

As it was, the tribesman avoided these, and took them to a narrow river, not much more than a large stream, that flowed along swiftly towards the mountain. This stream was almost completely covered in by bushes and trees that met above the water, making a kind of green tunnel, below which the river gurgled and bubbled.

'Wow! What an exciting river!' cried Jack, thrilled to see the dim green tunnel. 'How are we going to get along? Is it shallow enough to wade down the stream?'

'In parts it would be, but I don't fancy doing that,' said Pilescu. 'What is the fellow doing – and Mafumu too? I believe they are making rough rafts for us!'

'What fun!' cried Paul, and he ran to watch the two workers.

Mafumu was busy bringing armfuls of stuff that

looked rather like purple cork to his uncle. He had got it from a marshy piece of ground. It smelt horrible.

'Is it cork?' said Paul.

'No – it looks more like some sort of fungus, or enormous toadstool,' said Pilescu. 'Look at his uncle binding it together with creeper-ropes!'

In two hours' time four small rafts of the horrible-smelling material were made. They looked rather peculiar and they smelt even stranger, but they floated marvellously, bobbing about on the water like strange ducks. The children were delighted. It was going to be splendid fun to float down the hidden river, under a green archway of trees, right up to the Secret Mountain!

'Our guide says that his tribe always use these peculiar rafts to get quickly down this valley, which they fear because of the Mountain Folk,' said Ranni. 'The stream goes right round the foot of the Secret Mountain, and joins a river round there. Then it goes into the next valley, which is a fine hunting ground used by Mafumu's tribe. He says that the rafts don't last long – they gradually fall to bits – but last just long enough to take a man into the next valley with safety!'

Pilescu and Paul got on to one raft. It wobbled dangerously, but sank hardly at all into the water. There was only just room for the two of them to squat. They held on to the creeper-ropes that bound the raft together. Then down the stream they went, bobbing like corks.

Ranni and Nora went next. Mike and Peggy went together, and last of all came the guide, Jack, and, of course, Mafumu, who was determined not to leave Jack for even a minute!

It was a strange journey, a little frightening. The trees met overhead and were so thick that no sunlight pierced through to the swift stream. The only light there glowed a dim green.

'Your face looks green!' cried Peggy to Mike, as they set off together down the strange river-tunnel.

'So does yours!' said Mike. 'Everything looks green. I feel as if we must be under water! It's because we can't see any daylight at all – only the green of the trees and of the stream below.'

The stream became swifter as it ran down the valley. In no place did the trees break – the tunnel was complete the whole way. The rafts were really splendid, but towards the end of the journey they began to break up a little. The outside edges fell off, and the rafts began to loosen from the creeper-ropes.

'Hey! We shall soon be in the water!' yelled Ranni. 'Where do we land?'

The guide shouted something back. 'Well, that's a good thing!' cried Ranni. 'We're nearly there, children.'

The bobbing rafts spun slowly round and round as they went along. It really was a most peculiar journey, but the children loved every minute. They were sad to see their rafts gradually coming to pieces, getting smaller and smaller!

Suddenly the stream ran into a large still pool. It ran out again the other end of the pool, but when the guide gave a loud shout, everyone knew that their journey's end had come. The pool was their stopping place. If they went any further they would go right round the

mountain and into the next valley.

Ranni's raft spun into the quiet pool, and by pulling at the branches of a nearby tree he dragged himself and Nora to the bank, on which grew thick bushes. All the others followed, though Mike and Peggy nearly sailed right on, for their raft was right in the very middle of the current! However, they managed to swing it round and joined the others.

'If I don't get off my raft it will disappear from under me,' said big Ranni, whose weight had made his raft break up more than those of the others. Everyone jumped off their rafts and stood on the banks of the pool. They had to stand on rotting branches and roots, for the trees and bushes grew so thickly there that the bare ground could not be seen.

'Well – we've arrived,' said Pilescu. 'And now – where's the mountain? We should be at the foot.'

The guide, with a frown on his face, took them through the thick bushes, squeezing his way with difficulty, and came to a tall tree. He climbed it, beckoning the others behind him.

Ranni climbed up, and one by one everyone followed. They all wanted to see what the man had to show them. Monkeys fled chattering from the branches as the little company climbed upwards, helping themselves by using the long creepers which hung down like strong ropes.

Their guide took them almost to the top of the tree. It towered over the bush below, and from its top could be seen, quite close at hand, the Secret Mountain!

A Pleasant Surprise

The Secret Mountain towered up steeply. It was covered by the curious yellow bushes, which gave it its strange appearance from a distance. The bushes had yellow leaves and waxy-white flowers over which hovered brilliant butterflies and insects of every kind.

But it was the mountain itself that held the children's eyes. It was so steep. It looked quite impossible to climb. It rose up before their eyes, enormous, seeming to touch the sky. They were very near to it, and Nora was quite frightened by its bigness.

The tribesman frowned as he looked at it and muttered strings of weird-sounding words to himself. He was plainly going no further. Only the money he had been promised had made him come so far. He slid down the tree and spoke rapidly to Ranni.

Ranni told him where he would find his reward, and the man nodded, showing all his white teeth. He called to Mafumu, and the two of them disappeared into the bushes.

'Hey, Mafumu – say goodbye!' yelled Jack, very sorry indeed to see the merry little fellow going. But his uncle had Mafumu firmly by one ear and the boy could do nothing.

'Well, he might at least have said goodbye,' said

Peggy. 'I did like him. I wish he was going with us.'

'Did Mafumu's uncle give you any idea at all as to how we might get into the mountain?' Mike asked Ranni. Ranni shook his head.

'All he would say was that we should have to walk through the rock!' he said. 'I don't think he really knew what he meant. It was just something he had heard.'

'Walk through the rock!' said Jack. 'That sounds a bit like Ali Baba and the Forty Thieves. Do you remember – the robbers made their home in a cave inside a hill – and when the robber chief said, "Open Sesame!" a rock slid aside – and they all went in!'

Pilescu and Ranni did not know the tale, and they listened with interest.

'Well, the way in *may* be by means of a moving rock,' said Ranni. 'But, good gracious, we can't go all round this enormous mountain looking for a moving rock! And if we did find it, I'm sure we should not know the secret of moving it!'

They were all sitting down at the foot of the tree, eating a meal, for they were hungry and tired. It was hot in the valley, even in the shade of the trees. The calls of the birds, the hum of insects and the chattering of monkeys sounded all the time. The sun was sinking low, and Pilescu made up his mind that they must all camp where they were for the night. He glanced up at the enormous branches of the tree they were under, and wondered if, by spreading out the rugs in a big fork halfway up, the children could sleep there safely.

'I don't like letting the children sleep on the ground tonight,' he said to Ranni. 'I daren't light a fire to keep wild creatures away, because if we do we shall attract the attention of the Mountain Folk – and we don't want to be surrounded and captured in the night. Do you think that tree would hold them all?'

Ranni glanced upwards. The tree would hold them all right,' he said. 'But supposing they fall out in their sleep!'

'Oh, we can easily prevent that,' said Pilescu. 'We can tie them on with those creeper-ropes.'

The two men had been talking to one another in their own language, and only Paul understood. He listened with delight.

'We're going to sleep up in a tree!' he told the others, who listened in astonishment. 'We daren't light a fire tonight, you see.'

'Golly! How exciting!' said Mike. 'I really don't think anyone could have had such a lot of thrills in a short time as we've had this week!'

Pilescu made the children climb the tree whilst it was still daylight. Halfway up the branches forked widely, spreading out almost straight, and there was a kind of rough platform. Pilescu stuffed the spaces between the branches with creepers, twigs and some enormous leaves that he pulled from another tree. Then he spread out half the rugs, and told the children to settle down.

They spread themselves on the rugs, joyful to think they were to spend a whole night in a tree. Some monkeys, who had been watching from the next tree, set up a great chattering when they saw the children settling down.

'They think you are their cousins from a far-off land,'

said Pilescu with a broad grin. 'They're not far wrong, either. Now lie still whilst I cover you with these other rugs, and then I'm going to tie you firmly to the branches.'

'Oh, Pilescu – we're too hot to be covered!' cried Paul, pushing away the rug.

'It will be very chilly in the early morning,' said Pilescu. 'Very well – leave the rug half off now, and pull it on again later.'

Pilescu and Ranni made a very good job of tying the children to the tree. Now they were safe! The two men slid down the big tree to the ground. The monkeys fled away. The children talked drowsily for a while, and

Peggy tried her hardest to keep awake and enjoy the strangeness of a night up a tree.

But her eyes were very heavy, and although she listened for a while to the enormously loud voices of some giant frogs in the nearby marsh, and the curious call of a bird that seemed to say, 'Do do it, do do it,' over and over again, she was soon as fast asleep as the others.

As usual, Ranni and Pilescu took turn and turn about to watch. They both sat at the foot of the great tree, one at one side, the other at the other. Ranni took first turn, and then Pilescu.

Pilescu was very wide awake. He sat with his gun in his hand watching for any movement or sound nearby that might mean an enemy of some kind. He, too, heard the frogs, and the bird crying 'Do do it, do do it.' He heard the trumpeting of far-off elephants, the roar of some big forest cat, maybe a leopard, and the stir of the wind in the branches of the trees.

And then, towards dawn, he heard something and saw something that was not bird or animal. Something or someone was creeping between the bushes, very slowly, very carefully. Pilescu stiffened, and took hold of his gun firmly. Could it be any of the Folk of the Secret Mountain?

The Something came nearer, and Pilescu put out a hand and shook Ranni carefully. Ranni awoke at once.

'There's something strange over there,' whispered Pilescu. 'I can only see a shadow moving. Do you suppose it's a scout sent out by the Mountain Folk?'

Ranni peered between the bushes in the dim light of half-dawn. He, too, could see something moving.

'I'll slip behind that bush and pounce on whatever it is,' whispered Ranni. 'I can move away from this side of the tree without being seen.'

So big Ranni slid away as silently as a cat, and crawled behind the nearest bush. From there he made his way to another bush and waited for the Something to come by.

He pounced on it – and there came a terrified yell, and a shrill voice that cried out something that sounded like' Yakka, longa, yakka, longa!'

Ranni picked up what he had caught and carried it to Pilescu. It was something very small – something that both men knew very well. They cried out in amazement.

'Mafumu!'

Yes – it *was* Mafumu. Poor Mafumu, crawling painfully along the bushes, searching for the friends he had left the day before.

'Mafumu! What has happened?' asked Ranni. The boy told him his story.

'I went back a long way with my uncle, but he was unkind to me, and he told me he would give me to the first crocodile he saw in a river. So I ran away from him to come back to my new friends. And a big thorn went into my foot – see – so I could not walk, I could only crawl.'

The poor little boy was so tired, and in such pain that tears fell out of his eyes. As dawn came stealing over the countryside, big Ranni took the poor little fellow into his arms, whilst Pilescu pulled out the great thorn from his foot. He bathed the wound and bound it up with lint and gauze. He gave the boy something to eat and drink and then told him to sleep.

But comfortable though he was in Ranni's arms, Mafumu would not stay there. He must go to his new friends, and especially Jack!

So up the tree he climbed, and was soon snuggled down beside Jack, who did not even wake when the boy lay almost on top of him.

'Mafumu may be helpful to us,' said Pilescu to Ranni. 'He knows the language of the tribes around here, he knows where to find fruit and drinking water, and he can guide as well.'

In the morning, what loud cries of amazement came from the tree above, when the children awoke and found Mafumu with them!

'Mafumu!'

'How *did* you get here, Mafumu?'

'Mafumu, get off me, I can't move!'

'Mafumu, what have you done to your foot?'

Mafumu sat up on Jack's legs and grinned round happily.

'Me back,' he said, proud that he could say some English words with the right meaning. 'Me back.' Then he went off into his usual gibberish.

'Hello, goodnight, shutup, what's the matter!'

Everyone laughed. Jack punched him on the back in a friendly manner. 'You're an idiot, but an awfully nice idiot,' he said. 'We're jolly glad to see you again. I shouldn't be surprised if you help us quite a lot!'

And Jack was right, as we shall soon see!

The Wonderful Waterfall

As the little company sat eating their breakfast, they talked about what would be the best thing to do. How were they to find a way into the Secret Mountain?

'You know, I believe that Mafumu's uncle knew something,' said Ranni. 'I rather think there is some sort of secret way in, if only we could find it.'

'Ranni! I know how we could find it!' said Mike excitedly. 'Couldn't we hide until we see some of the Secret Mountain Folk – and then track them to see how they get inside?'

'Yes – if we could only see some of the folk, without them seeing us!' said Ranni. 'We should have to scout round a bit – it is perfectly plain that no one could possibly get into the mountain from *this* side – it's so steep. I don't believe even a goat could get up it!'

'Well – let's explore round the other side,' said Mike. 'Hurry up and finish your breakfast, girls. I can hardly wait.'

'Of course, you realize that we shall all have to be very careful,' said Pilescu. 'It is quite possible that the folk in the Secret Mountain already know we are here, and are waiting to capture us.'

'Oooh,' said Nora, not liking the sound of that at all. 'I shall keep very near to you and Ranni, Pilescu!'

'I hope you will,' said Pilescu, taking the little girl's hand in his. 'I would not have come on this mad adventure if I had known what it was to be. But now it is too late to draw back.'

'I should think so!' cried Mike indignantly. 'Why, Pilescu, things are going very well, I think. We have discovered where our parents are – and we may be able to rescue them at any time now.'

'Yes – but first we have to find where your parents are!' said Pilescu. 'And how to get to them.'

'Well, let's make a start,' said Mike. 'Come on. It will be too hot soon to explore anywhere! All my clothes are sticking to me already.'

The party packed up their things. Ranni and Pilescu carried most of them, but the children had to take some too. Mafumu as usual carried his share balanced on his head. They all set off cautiously, keeping as near to the foot of the steep mountain as they could, and yet taking cover as they went, so as not to be seen.

It was difficult going. Mafumu was a great help, for he seemed to know the best paths at once. He went in front, with Ranni and Jack just behind him. Pilescu was at the back, his hand on his gun. He was taking no risks!

As they went round the mountain a strange noise came to their ears.

'What's that?' said Nora, alarmed. They all stood and listened. Mafumu beckoned them on, not knowing why they had stopped.

'Big noise, Mafumu, big noise,' said Jack, holding up his hand for Mafumu to listen. The boy laughed.

'Big water,' he said. 'Big water.' He was very proud of himself for being able to answer Jack in his own language. He was as sharp as a needle, and in half an hour was quite able to pick up twenty or more new words.

'Big water!' said Jack puzzled. 'Does he mean the sea?'

'No – I know what it is – it's a waterfall!' said Mike. 'Listen! It sounds like thunder, but it's really water tumbling down the mountainside not far off. Come on – I bet I'm right.'

The little company pressed on, following their new guide. The noise grew louder. It really did sound like thunder, but was more musical. The echoes went rolling round the valley, and now and again the noise seemed to get inside the children's heads in a strange manner. They shook their heads to get it out! It was funny.

And then they suddenly saw the waterfall! It was simply magnificent. It fell almost straight down the steep mountainside with a tremendous noise. Spray rose high into the air, and hung like a mist over the fall. The children could feel its wetness on their faces now and again from where they stood, awed and silent at the sight of such a wonderful fall of water.

'My goodness!' said Peggy, full of astonishment and delight. 'No wonder it makes such a noise! It's a *marvellous* waterfall. It's coming from the inside of the mountain!'

'Yes – it is,' said Mike, shading his eyes and looking upwards. 'There must be an underground river that wanders through the mountain and comes out at that steep place. How are we going to get by?'

It was very difficult. They had to go a good way out

of their path. The waterfall made a surging, violent river at its foot, that shouted and tumbled its way down the valley, and joined the hidden river down which they had come not long before.

Mafumu was not to be beaten by a waterfall! He made his way alongside the surging water until he came to a shallow part, where big boulders stuck up all the way across.

'Hurryup, hurryup,' he said, pointing to the stones. 'We go there, hurryup.'

'I believe we *could* get across there,' said Ranni. 'The stones are almost like stepping-stones. I will carry Nora across, and then Peggy – and you take Paul, Pilescu. The boys can manage themselves.'

'*I* can manage by *myself*,' said the little Prince indignantly. 'I'm a boy too, aren't I?'

'You are not so big as the others,' said Pilescu with a grin, and he caught up the angry boy and put him firmly on his shoulder. Paul was red with rage, but he did not dare to struggle in case he sent Pilescu into the water. As it was, Pilescu lost his footing once, and almost fell. He just managed to swing himself back in time, and sat with a bump on a big rock. Paul was almost jerked off his shoulder.

The girls were taken safely across. As Ranni had said, the stones were almost like stepping-stones, although one or two were rather far apart – but fortunately the water there was only waist-deep, so a little wading solved the difficulty. The other three boys got across easily. Mafumu jumped like a goat from one stone to another.

And now they were the other side of the waterfall.

The noise of its falling still sounded thunderous, but they liked it.

'The foam is like soap-suds,' said Nora, watching some swirling down the river.

The sun was now too high for any of them to go further. Even Mafumu was hot and wanted to rest. Also his foot pained him a little now, in spite of the careful bandaging. Everyone curled up in the cool shade of an enormous tree, where they could occasionally feel the delicious coldness of the misty spray from the waterfall.

'I suppose we ought to have a meal,' said Ranni, too lazy to do anything about it.

'I'm so hot and tired I couldn't eat even an ant's egg!' said Jack.

'You haven't been offered one,' said Peggy. 'The only thing *I'd* like would be something sweet to drink.'

Mafumu disappeared for a moment. He came back laden with some strange-looking fruit, that looked like half nut, half pomegranate. He slit a hole in the top-end and showed Peggy how to drink from it.

'I suppose it's safe to drink the juice of this funny fruit,' said Peggy doubtfully.

Ranni nodded. 'Mafumu knows what is good or not,' he said. 'Taste it and see what it's like. If it's nice I'll have some too!'

Peggy tipped up the strange green fruit. It was full of some thick, fleshy juice that trickled out rather like treacle. At first the taste was bitter, like lemon – but as the little girl sucked hard, a delicious coolness spread over her mouth and down her throat.

'Gosh!' said Peggy. 'It makes me feel as if I've got ice-cream going down me, but not at all sweet. Do have some, you others!'

Soon everyone was sucking the strange fruit. Nobody liked the bitter taste at first, but they all loved the glorious coolness that came afterwards.

'Mafumu, you are very, very clever,' said Jack sleepily to the little boy, who was, as usual, curled up as near to his hero as he could manage. Mafumu grinned in delight. A word of praise from Jack made him very happy.

Soon everyone was sleeping soundly – except Ranni, who was on guard, though he found it very difficult to keep awake in such heat. The heat danced round, and everything shimmered and quivered. If it had not been for the coolness that blew over from the nearby waterfall it would have been quite unbearable.

Even the monkeys were quiet – but when they began to move in the tree and to chatter again Ranni awoke everyone. The great heat of the day was gone. If they were going to do any more exploring they must set off at once.

And soon they had a great surprise – for when they rounded a rocky corner of the yellow mountain they heard voices! They all stopped still at once, hardly daring to breathe. Voices! Could they be natives – or folk from the Mountain?

The voices were deep and harsh – like the voices of rooks, Jack thought. Ranni waved Mafumu forward, for he knew that the boy could move as silently as a shadow. Mafumu slid down on to his tummy and wriggled forward like a snake. It was marvellous to watch. The other children could not imagine how he could get along as quickly as he did.

Everyone else sank down quietly behind the bushes and stayed as still as mice. Mafumu wriggled forward into a thick bush. It was prickly, but the boy did not seem to feel the scratches. He parted the bush-twigs carefully and looked through.

Then he looked back towards Ranni, his face full of excitement, and beckoned him forward with a wave of his hand. The children had the amusement of watching big Ranni do his best to wriggle forward on his front, just as Mafumu had done. The enormous Baronian did very well, however, and was soon beside the boy, peering through the prickly bush.

The two of them stayed there for some time. The others waited impatiently, hearing the harsh voices of the strangers, and wondering what Ranni and Mafumu could see.

Suddenly there came a grating sound, a rolling, groaning noise – and the voices stopped. The weird noise came again, such a grating sound that it set everyone's teeth on edge! With the rolling sound of rumbling thunder the noise echoed around – and then stopped. Now only the sharp calls of the birds, the ceaseless hum of thousands of insects and the silly chatter of monkeys could be heard – and behind it all the roaring of the waterfall in the distance.

Ranni and Mafumu crawled back, their faces shining with excitement. They took hold of the other children and hurried them to a safe distance. And in the shade of a great rock Ranni told them what he and Mafumu had seen.

The Way into the Secret Mountain

'Quick, Ranni, tell us everything!' said Jack.

'We saw some of the Folk of the Secret Mountain!' said Ranni. 'They certainly do look weird. It is just as Mafumu's uncle said – they have flaming red hair and beards and their skins are a funny yellow. I couldn't see if their eyes were green. They were dressed in flowing robes of all colours, and they wore turbans that showed their red hair.'

'Golly!' said Mike, his eyes wide with excitement. 'Go on – what happened?'

'The most peculiar thing happened,' said Ranni. 'I hardly know if I believe it or not. Well – let me tell you. As we lay there, watching these people talking together in their funny harsh voices, we noticed that they were near a very curious kind of rock.'

'What sort of rock?' asked Pilescu.

'It was an enormous rock,' said Ranni. 'It was strange because it was much smaller at the bottom than at the top, so that it looked almost as if it must fall over. Well, as we watched, one of the Mountain Folk went up to the rock and pushed hard against it.'

'Why, he couldn't surely move an enormous rock!' cried Mike.

'That's what *I* thought,' said Ranni. 'But that rock

must be one of these curious balancing rocks that can be pivoted, or swung round, at a touch, no matter how big they are. There are just a few known in the world, and this is another.'

'What happened when the rock swung round?' asked Pilescu.

'It not only swung round, it slid to one side,' said Ranni. 'Just like the rock in the story of Ali Baba that you told me! And behind it was a great door in the mountainside studded with shining knobs that glittered in the sun!'

Everyone stared at Ranni in silence, too excited to speak. So that was the way into the mountain! They had stumbled on it quite by accident.

'Go on,' whispered Peggy at last.

'I couldn't see how the great doorway was opened,' said Ranni. 'It seemed to slide to one side, very quietly – but whether it was opened from the outside or the inside I really don't know. Then the rock rolled back into place again, and swung back into position with that terrific roaring, groaning sound you heard.'

'And did the people go into the mountain?' asked Mike.

'They did,' answered Ranni. 'We saw no more of them.'

Everyone sat silent for a while, thinking of the strange entrance to the Secret Mountain. So that was what Mafumu's uncle had meant when he said that to get into the mountain one had to walk through rock!

'Well – what are we going to do?' said Jack. 'We know the way in – but I wonder how that great studded door is opened! Oh, Ranni – can we try to get in tonight?'

'We'd better,' said Ranni. 'I will try by myself and see what happens. You can all find good hiding-places nearby and watch. I'll take my gun, you may be sure!'

The children could hardly wait for the sudden nightfall to come. They found themselves good hiding-places – though Jack and Mafumu found the best. Theirs was up a big tree not far from the mountain entrance. Mafumu found it, of course, and helped Jack up there. The others were behind or in the middle of thick bushes.

When the stars hung brightly, and a crescent moon shone in the sky, Ranni crept forward to the strange rock, whose black shadow was enormous in the night. Everyone watched, hardly daring to breathe in case anything happened to Ranni.

Big Ranni stepped quietly up to the rock. He thought he knew exactly where to heave, for he had seen one of the Mountain Folk move the rock and had noted the exact place. But it was difficult to find it at night.

Ranni shoved and pushed. He pressed against the rock and heaved with all his might. Nothing happened. He stopped and mopped his hot forehead, wondering which was the right place to press against.

He tried again and again – and just as he was giving up something happened. He pushed at the right place quite by accident! With a groaning roar the enormous rock swung slowly round and then slid back. The noise it made was terrific. Ranni sprang back into the shadows, afraid that a hundred Mountain Folk might come rushing out at him.

The studded door shone in the moonlight. It did not open. It stood there, big and solid, strange and silent, barring the way. Nobody came. Nobody shouted to see who had swung back the rock. Only the night sounds came on the air, and the sound of the distant waterfall.

Everyone waited, trembling with excitement. Jack nearly fell out of his tree, he shivered so much with wonder and expectation. But absolutely nothing happened. The rock remained where it was, the door shone behind.

'Ranni! Maybe the Mountain Folk haven't heard the noise!' whispered Pilescu. 'Go and try the door.'

Ranni crept forward again, keeping to the deep-black shadows. Once or twice the moonlight glinted on the gun he held in his hand. Ranni was taking no chances!

The others watched him from their hiding-places. He went right up to the door. He felt over it with his hand. He pushed gently against it. He tried to slide it to one side. He tried all the studs and knobs to see if by chance any of them opened the great door. But no matter what he did, the door remained shut.

'Let us come and see,' whispered Mike to Pilescu. The boy felt that he could not keep still any longer. Pilescu was also longing to go to the mountain door, so he, Mike, Paul, and the two girls crept forward in the shadows.

Jack wanted to come too – and began to climb carefully down the tree, getting caught in a great creeper as he did so. Mafumu tried to untangle him, but the more he tried, the more mixed-up poor Jack got.

And then, just as Jack was almost untangled, there

came a grinding, grating roar once more – and the enormous rock slid along in front of the great door and swung round slowly into its place.

Behind it, caught between the rock and the door, was everyone except Mafumu and Jack! The girls, Mike, Paul, Ranni and Pilescu were in the narrow passage between.

Ranni tried to stop the rock from sliding back into place, but once started on its way nothing would stop the enormously heavy rock. No one could escape, either, for there was no time to slip out of the trap.

Jack and Mafumu stared towards the rock in the greatest dismay. Jack leapt down from the tree, almost breaking his ankle, and ran towards the mountain.

'Are you safe, are you safe!' he shouted.

But there was no answer. The swinging rock shut the sound of voices away. Jack beat on the rock, he tried to heave it as he had seen Ranni do, and Mafumu did the same. But neither boy could find the secret balance of the rock, and it stayed where it was, colossal in the moonlight, towering above them as they shouted and hammered on it.

And then, behind the rock, the great door slid back! Jack and Mafumu heard it, and fell silent, listening. What was happening?

What indeed? When the door slid back, the little company in front of it stared with wide eyes into a great hall-like cave. It was lighted by glowing lamps, and a wide flight of steps led downwards for a little way. Up these steps came the Folk of the Secret Mountain, dressed in their flowing robes, and carrying strange yellow wands which glittered from top to bottom.

The leader was a very tall man with a bright red beard and gleaming eyes. He spoke to Ranni in language rather like that used by Mafumu. Ranni understood some of it.

'He wants us to follow him,' Ranni said to Pilescu. 'Got your gun, Pilescu?'

'Yes,' said the big Baronian. 'But it's no use using it, Ranni. There are too many of them. Put your gun away for the moment, and we'll see what happens. We are in a nice mess now. Only Jack and Mafumu are safe!'

That was a strange journey into the heart of the mountain. Big carved lamps glowed all the way, lighting up enormous flights of steps, great walls, and high rocky ceilings.

'The mountain is full of hollows which these people have made into halls and rooms,' said Ranni in a low voice to Pilescu. 'Isn't it amazing? Look at those great pictures drawn in colour on the walls! They are strange but very beautiful.'

The children gazed in wonder at the great coloured pictures on the rocky walls of the mountain caves. Lamps were set cleverly to light up the pictures so that the men and animals in them seemed almost alive. The Secret Mountain was indeed a marvellous place!

At last the long journey through the heart of the mountain came to an end. The little party found themselves in a strange room, whose rocky ceiling rose too high for them to make out by the light of their lamp. Shining stones were set into the walls, and these glittered like stars in the lamplight.

A rough platform was at one end of the room. On it

were piled heaps of wonderful rugs, beautifully woven, and marvellously patterned in all the brightest colours imaginable. The children sat down on them, tired out.

Pitchers of ice-cold water stood on a stone table. Everyone drank deep. Flat cakes lay on a shallow dish beside the pitchers. Mike tasted one. It was sweet and dry, quite pleasant to eat. Everyone made a meal, wondering what was going to happen.

The door to their strange room was made of strong wood and had been fastened on the outside. There was nothing to do but wait. The Mountain Folk had left them quite alone in the heart of their peculiar home.

'We'd better get some rest,' said Ranni, and he covered up the three children with the rugs. 'I don't know what

to wish about Jack. I'm glad he's not caught – and yet I wish we were all here together.'

'Perhaps Jack and Mafumu will find some way of rescuing us,' said Peggy hopefully.

Ranni laughed shortly. 'It's no good hoping that, Peggy! If he tries to get through the rock entrance, and through that big studded door, he will just find himself a prisoner!'

'Do you suppose we'll see Mummy and Daddy?' asked Nora suddenly. 'They must be somewhere in this mountain too.'

'Yes – that's quite likely,' said Pilescu thoughtfully. 'Ranni, I'll keep guard for the first half of the night. You go to sleep with the others now.'

In spite of all the tremendous excitement of the day the three children were soon asleep on the soft rugs. Ranni did not sleep at first, but at last he dozed off, sitting half upright in case Pilescu needed him quickly.

But the night passed away silently and no one came to

disturb them in their cell-like room. The lamp burned steadily, giving a soft light to the curious, high-roofed room. It burned until the day – and even then it still lit the room, for no daylight, no sunlight ever entered the heart of the Secret Mountain.

Mafumu Makes a Discovery

Jack was almost beside himself with alarm and despair. Mafumu kept close beside him, saying nothing at all, looking at Jack out of his big dark eyes. Both boys beat again and again on the great rock that hid the entrance to the Secret Mountain. They heard the door behind slide back into place once more – and then all was silent.

'Come,' said Mafumu at last, and he took Jack's arm. He led him to where everyone had left their packs, and the two sat down together.

'What are we to do?' said Jack at last, burying his head in his hands. 'I can't bear to think of everyone captured, and we can't get at them.'

Mafumu did not understand. He sat there looking at Jack, muttering something in his own language. Then he made a kind of bed of the packs, and pushed Jack down on them.

'We sleep now. I find way soon,' said the younger boy flashing his white teeth in the moonlight. They must wait until the morning.

Jack fell asleep at last. As soon as Mafumu saw that his eyes were closed, and heard his regular breathing he crept away from Jack. He stood upright in the brilliant moonlight and looked at the great mountain. How was he going to find a way inside?

Mafumu was not yet ten years old, but he was the sharpest boy in his tribe. He was mischievous, disobedient and wilful, but he had brains. He had lain thinking and thinking of how he might get into the Secret Mountain without going through the entrance of the sliding rock.

And into his mind had come a picture of the great waterfall. He saw it springing from the mountainside, a great gushing fall of silvery water. He was going to see if it came from the heart of the Secret Mountain!

The boy slipped away in the moonlight. He ran until he came to the great waterfall. It was magnificent in the light of the moon, and the spray shone like purest silver. The noise was twice as loud at night, and he was half afraid.

He glanced fearfully all round him. He was not afraid of animals or snakes – but he was afraid of being caught by the Folk of the Mountain. If he should be captured, Jack would be left helpless, for he did not know the countryside as Mafumu did.

Mafumu made his way up the mountain, keeping as close to the waterfall as he could. Several times he was drenched, but he liked that. It was cool! The night was hot, and Mafumu was bathed in perspiration as he climbed upwards. The mountain was very steep indeed. It was only by working his way from rocky ledge to ledge that he could get up at all.

At last he came to where the waterfall began. Mafumu worked his way above the fall, and found that, as he had thought, the water gushed straight out of the mountain itself. There must be an underground river running through the mountain. The great hill towered above him, reaching to the clouds. Just below him the waterfall sprang from the mountain, and the fine spray clung to his skin.

He worked his way down again, almost defeated by the noise of the fall. He came to where the water shot out of the mountain in a great arch. He wriggled his way towards it, and found a rocky ledge, wide and damp, just by the fall itself.

Mafumu stood and shivered with fright, for the noise was tremendous. It flowed all around him like rumbling thunder. He edged his way behind the great arch of water, for the rocky ledge stretched all the way behind.

And there, hidden in the misty spray that hung always around and about the waterfall, Mafumu thought that he had discovered another way into the Secret Mountain! For surely, where the water was able to come out of the mountain, he and Jack would be able to go in!

The moon was now almost gone, and darkness crept across the country. Mafumu shivered. He had a curious charm round his neck, made of crocodile teeth, and he took it into his hand to bring him good luck. He slid quickly down the mountainside, grazing himself as he went, and bruising his ankle-bones as he knocked them against rocks and stones. But he did not even feel the pain, so anxious was he to get back to Jack, and tell him what he had found.

He reached Jack as the dawn was breaking. Jack was awake, and very puzzled because Mafumu was gone. The boy looked white and worried. He simply had no idea at all what would be the best thing to do. He had almost made up his mind that he must try to move the rock somehow and get into the mountain so as to be with the others.

But Mafumu had other plans. In funny, broken English he tried to explain to Jack what his idea was.

'Big, big water,' he said, and made a noise like the splashing of the waterfall. 'Jack come with Mafumu see big, big water. We go into big, big water. Come.'

Jack thought Mafumu was quite mad, but the other boy was so much in earnest that he nodded his head and said Yes, he would come.

Leaving their packs where they were, covered by boulders and stones, the two boys made their way back to the great waterfall. The noise was so deafening that they had to shout to one another to make themselves heard.

Mafumu remembered the way he had taken in the moonlight. He never forgot any path he had once travelled. He even remembered the bushes and rocks he had passed. So now he found it easy to help Jack up the rocky ledges to where the water gushed out of the mountainside.

Jack was wet through and almost deaf by the time he reached the place where the water appeared from the mountain. He kept shaking his head to get the noise of the fall out of it – but it was impossible! It went on all the time.

Mafumu was excited. He led Jack behind the great curve of the fall, and showed him how the water thundered out just above their heads. It was an odd feeling to stand immediately under a great waterfall, and see it pouring down overhead and in front, a great

blue-green mass of water, powerful enough to sweep the boys off and away if it could have reached them!

'How weird to stand behind a waterfall like this,' said Jack. 'Mafumu – what's the sense of bringing me here? How do you suppose we're going to crawl through water that's coming out of the mountain at about sixty miles an hour. You must be mad.'

But Mafumu was not mad. He took Jack right to the other side of the ledge, and pointed to a narrow rocky path that led into the mountain, where the water ran only two or three inches deep. Nearby, the river had worn a deep channel for itself – but this ledge was just above the level of the river, and had water on it only because of the continual splashing and spray that came from the fall.

'We go in here,' grinned Mafumu. 'We go in here, yes?'

'Gosh, Mafumu – I believe you are right!' said Jack, excited. 'I believe we can go in here! Though goodness knows how far we'll get, or where it will take us.'

'We go now,' said Mafumu. 'Hurryup, hurryup.'

The boys squeezed themselves on to the rocky ledge. If they had slipped into the great torrent of water that poured out, that would have been the end of them. But they were careful to hold on to bits of jutting-out rock, so as not to fall. The ledge was damp and slippery. The air was full of fine spray. It was strange to be squeezing by a great river that became a waterfall two or three feet away from them!

The rocky ledge ran right into the mountain, keeping a foot or two above the level of the deep hidden river. The boys made their way along it. Soon they had left behind the thunder of the waterfall, and the mountain seemed strangely silent. Just below them, to their left, ran the underground river, silent and swift.

'It's dark, Mafumu,' said Jack, shivering. It was not only dark, but cold. No sunshine ever came up the secret river! But soon a peculiar light showed from the roof and walls of the river tunnel.

It shone green and blue. Mafumu thought it was very odd, but Jack knew that it was only the strange light called phosphorescence. He was glad of its pale gleam, for now they could see more or less where they were going.

'We shan't fall down into the river now and be swept out into the waterfall,' he thought. 'My goodness, Mafumu was clever to think there might be a way into the mountain, where the river came out and made a fall! I should never have thought of that in a hundred years! Wouldn't it be marvellous if we could rescue everyone!'

After a long crawl along the ledge the tunnel opened out into a series of caves, some large, some small. The boys marvelled at some of them, for the walls were agleam with bright shiny stones. Mafumu did not like them.

'The walls have eyes that look at Mafumu,' he whispered to Jack. Jack laughed – but he soon stopped, for his laugh echoed round and round the caves, and rumbled into the heart of the mountain and came back to him like a hundred giant-laughs, very eerie and horrible.

On through the river caves went the two boys, silent and rather frightened now. Then they came to what seemed a complete stop.

'Mafumu! The river is in a tunnel here, and the roof almost touches the top of the water!' said Jack in dismay. 'We can't get any further.'

Mafumu waded into the river. It was not running very swiftly just there, for it was almost on the level. It was deep, however, and the boy had to swim. He began to make his way up the tunnel to see how far he could go with his head above the water. His head knocked against the roof as he swam – and presently he found that the water touched the roof! So he had to swim under the water, and hoped that before he choked the roof would rise a little and give him air to breathe!

Mafumu was a good swimmer, and was able to hold his breath well – but his lungs were almost bursting by the time that he was able to find a place to stick up his head above the water and breathe again. Even so, the roof fell low again almost at once, and the water bobbed against it. How far would it be before it rose again and Mafumu could breathe?

He had to try. There was nothing else to do, unless he and Jack were to go right back. So he took an enormous breath, dived down and swam vigorously below the water, trying the roof with his hand every now and again to see if he could come above the water and breathe.

He was rewarded. The roof suddenly rose up and the tunnel became a large cave! Mafumu waded out of the water gasping and panting, delighted that he had not given up too soon!

He sat down for a few minutes to get all the breath he could. He had to go back and bring Jack through now!

He did not know if the other boy could swim under water as well as he, Mafumu, could!

Back went Mafumu, knowing exactly where to rise and breathe, and where to dive under and swim back to where Jack was anxiously awaiting him, wondering what in the wide world had happened!

Mafumu tried to explain to Jack what he was to do. Jack understood only too well!

'Lead on, Mafumu,' said the boy, taking a deep breath. 'I'm a good swimmer – but I don't know if I'm as good as you are! Go on!'

So into the river went both boys, swimming below the water where it touched the roof, and coming up, almost bursting, in the place where the roof lifted a little so that they might breathe.

Then into the water they went again, shivering, for it was icy-cold, and once more swam as fast as they could up the low tunnel, their heads bumping the roof till they came thankfully to where the tunnel opened out into the large cave! They crawled out of the water, panting, and sat down to get their breath. Their hearts beat like great pumps, and it was some time before both boys could go on.

'Now which way?' wondered Jack, looking all round at the gleaming cave. There are three or four archways leading out of this cave, Mafumu, with the river winding silently through the middle. Which way do we go?'

Inside the Mountain

Mafumu was running all round, peering first through one rocky archway and then through another. He stopped at last and beckoned to Jack. Jack went over to him, wondering what the other boy could see, for he was plainly excited.

No wonder Mafumu was excited! Peering through the little archway he had seen an enormous flight of steps leading upwards through the mountain! The steps were cut out of the solid rock, and were polished and shining. At the foot hung a great lamp, very finely made, which gave a curious green light.

The boys stood at the bottom of the rocky stairway, staring upwards. Where could it lead to?

'Shall we go up?' whispered Jack, his whisper starting a rustling echo all around him. Mafumu nodded. In silence the two boys began to climb the great stairway. It went up for a great way, wide and easy to climb. Then it curved sharply to the right and became a curious spiral staircase, still cut into the rock.

'I believe it leads up to the top of the mountain!' said Jack, quite out of breath. 'Let's sit down and have a rest. My legs are really tired with all this climbing.'

They did not notice that a wooden door opened on to the stairway just behind them. They sat there in silence, resting themselves. And then suddenly they heard the harsh voices of the Folk of the Mountain! The boys looked round quickly and by the light of one of the green lamps hanging at a curve of the stairway they saw the door. It was just opening!

The boys did not know whether the folk would go up the stairway or down, and they hadn't time to choose! They simply tumbled themselves down the steps, came to a curve and waited there, their hearts thumping, and their legs trembling.

'If they come down the stairway we shall be seen!' thought Jack desperately. 'They will touch us as they pass, because the stairway is so narrow.'

But the Folk of the Mountain went *up* the stairway, not down! The boys heard their footsteps and their voices disappearing into the distance. They crept back up the stairway to the door – and it was open!

'Gosh! What a bit of luck!' Jack whispered to Mafumu, who, although he did not understand the words, knew what Jack meant all right. The boys slipped in through the open door and found themselves in an enormous gallery that ran round the most colossal hall they had ever seen.

'This must be a kind of meeting-hall,' thought Jack, gazing down from the rocky gallery to the great floor below. 'I bet it's right in the very middle of the mountain! What a strange place it is!'

Steps led up from the great hall in many directions. They led to fine wooden doors, studded and starred with gleaming metals. The Folk of the Mountain had a strange and mighty home! There was no one at all to be seen and the deep silence seemed very eerie. Enormous lamps hung down from the roof, swinging slightly as they burned. Deep shadows moved over the floor as the lamps swung, and Mafumu stared, for he had never seen such a place in all his life.

'Mafumu! Those people will be coming back soon, I expect,' said Jack in his ear. 'Come on. We must get down into this hall and go up a stairway to see if we can find where the others are. Hurry!'

The boys slipped down into the great hall. They stood there in the shadows, wondering which flight of steps to take. They chose the nearest one, a wide, shallow stretch that led to an open doorway.

Up they went, and through the doorway. A long, dark passage lay before them, with rocky walls and ceiling. They went down it, and turned into another one. They heard the noise of voices and stopped.

No one had heard them, so they crept on again, and came out through a big archway that led into a fine cave. Its walls were hung with the skins of animals and with curtains of shining material. The floor was covered with rich rugs. On them sat the Folk of the Secret Mountain.

How weird they looked in the light of the swinging lamps! The men all had flaming red beards and hair, and their faces looked a sickly yellow. The women were wrapped up to their noses, and showed neither hair nor chins! The boys knew they were the women because they spoke in high-pitched, shrill voices.

All of them were working at something. Some were making rugs. Others were weaving with bright-coloured

strands that looked like raffia. Some were hammering at things that the boys could not see.

'We'd better go back,' whispered Jack, pushing Mafumu. 'Come on. If we're seen here we'd be taken prisoner.'

The boys crept back. Mafumu was frightened, for the Folk of the Mountain had looked so strange! The two boys went back until they came to another door. It was shut. They pushed against it and it opened.

The room inside was very odd. It held nothing at all but a rope ladder that went up and up and up into the darkness of the roof!

'There must be a narrow hole that goes up for a long

way,' whispered Jack. 'I wonder where the rope ladder leads to. Sh! Mafumu – there's someone coming!'

Sure enough, voices and footsteps could be heard once more. Mafumu gave a groan of fright, caught hold of the rope ladder, and was up it in a flash, disappearing into the darkness of the high roof at once. Jack thought it was a good idea and he followed as well.

Just in time! Three men came into the little room, shut the door and began to talk in their harsh voices. Jack and Mafumu stayed still on the ladder, for they knew that if they climbed higher the ladder would shake and the men would guess someone was up there.

The men talked for ten minutes, and then went out. The two boys climbed up the ladder at once. They thought they would be safer at the top than at the bottom!

The ladder was fastened to a ledge, and opposite the ledge was another door, strong and heavy. It was bolted on the outside with great heavy bolts that looked impossible to move!

'Somebody's bolted in there,' whispered Jack. 'Do you suppose it's Peggy and Nora and Mike and the rest of them?'

Mafumu nodded. Yes – he felt sure they had stumbled on the prison of the rest of their little party! He began to pull at the bolts.

Although they were heavy, they were well oiled and ran fairly easily when both boys pulled at them. One by one they slid them back. There was a kind of latch on the door, and Jack slid it up. The door opened.

Not a sound came from the room inside. The boys

hardly dared to peep round the door. What would they see? Surely if their friends were in there they would have made some sound, said something or shouted something!

Jack pushed the door wide open and went boldly inside, far more boldly than he felt! And what a surprise he got!

The rest of their party were not there – but Captain and Mrs Arnold were! They lay on piles of rugs in the corner of the dimly lit cave, looking pale and ill. They watched the opening of the door, thinking that someone was bringing them food.

When they saw Jack they sprang to their feet in the greatest amazement! They stared as if they could not believe their eyes. They felt they must be dreaming.

'Jack! Jack! Is it really you?' asked Mrs Arnold at last. 'Where are the others – Mike, Peggy and Nora?'

Mike, Peggy and Nora were Mrs Arnold's own children, though she counted Jack as hers too, because he had once helped the others when they were in great trouble. Jack stared at Captain and Mrs Arnold in joy. He flung his arms round Mrs Arnold, for he was very fond of her.

'There isn't time to talk,' said Captain Arnold quickly. 'Jack has opened our prison door. We'd better get out whilst we have the chance! Follow me. I know where we can go and talk in safety.'

He led the way out of the room, taking with him some flat cakes and a pitcher of water. He stopped to fasten the bolts behind him, so that anyone coming that way would not notice anything unusual. Then, instead of going down the rope ladder, Captain Arnold took a little dark passage to the right that led steeply upwards. Before very long, much to the two boys' amazement, they came into a vivid patch of sunlight!

'There are sun-windows cut into the steep sides of this mountain here and there,' said Captain Arnold. 'The Folk of the Mountain use them for sunbathing. It is impossible to escape through them because the mountain falls away below them, and anyone squeezing out of a sun-window would roll to the bottom at once! We are safe here. Sometimes my wife and I have been taken here to get a bit of sun, and no one ever comes by.'

'Tell us everything, Jack,' begged Mrs Arnold. 'Quick – what about the others?'

Jack and Mafumu were very glad indeed to curl up in the warm sunshine and feel the light and warmth of the sun once more. They munched the cakes and drank the water whilst Jack quickly told his whole story. Captain and Mrs Arnold listened in the greatest astonishment.

'Well, you have had amazing adventures before – but, really, this is the most extraordinary one you children have yet had!' said Captain Arnold. 'And now, let me tell you our adventures!'

He told them how he had been forced down to mend something that had gone wrong with the White Swallow. Whilst he was mending it, the Folk of the Mountain had come silently up and captured them. They had been taken off to the secret mountain, and had been kept prisoners ever since.

'We don't exactly know why,' said Captain Arnold.

'But I'm afraid that the Folk of the Mountain don't mean us any good! They are worshippers of the sun, and I believe they have a great temple yard up on the top of this mountain where they make sacrifices to the sun. I only hope they don't mean to throw us over the mountain top to please the sun-god, or something like that!'

'Good gracious!' said Jack, going pale. He had read in history books of ancient tribes who had worshipped strange gods and made sacrifices to them. He had never dreamed it could happen today. 'What about the others? Will the Mountain Folk do that sort of thing to them too?'

'Well, we must see that they don't,' said Captain Arnold.

'The others are in the mountain somewhere – and we must find them! Have you finished your cakes, Jack? Well, we will leave this warm sun-trap now and explore a little. I don't expect anyone will find out that we are gone until the morning, as our guards had already brought us our food for the day. We have a good many hours to hunt for the others!'

At first Mafumu was very shy of the two strange people, but when he saw how Jack chattered to them he soon began grinning and showing his white teeth.

'Me Mafumu,' he said. 'Me Mafumu. Me Jack's friend!'

'Well, come on, Mafumu. You must keep with us,' said Captain Arnold. 'Follow me along this passage, and we'll see where it leads us to!'

On the Top of the Mountain

Meanwhile, what had happened to the others? They had slept restlessly in their underground room, with the lamp burning beside them. They only knew when morning came because their watches told them that it was six o'clock.

'I'm hungry,' said Mike, yawning. 'I hope they give their prisoners plenty to eat in this Secret Mountain!'

No sooner had he spoken than the door was unbolted and two red-haired men came in, the folds of their brightly coloured robes swishing all around them. They carried fresh water and some more of the flat cakes in a big dish. They also brought fruit of all kinds, which the children were delighted to see.

'I do wonder what has happened to Jack and Mafumu,' said Mike. 'What will they do, do you think, Ranni?'

'I can't imagine,' said Ranni, taking some of the fruit. He and Pilescu were far more worried than they would tell the children. They hated the sight of the weird red-haired folk – though both Ranni and Pilescu looked curiously like them sometimes, with their bright red hair and beards. But their eyes were not green, nor was their skin yellow.

Towards the end of the long and boring day, the door was flung open, and one of their guards beckoned the little company out. They followed their guide down long, winding passages, cut out of the mountain rock itself, and at last came to a great door that shone green and blue in the light of the swinging lamps above.

The door slid to one side as they came near it, and behind it the children saw a great flight of steps going up and up. The steps shone with a strange golden colour, and shimmered from orange to yellow as the little company began to climb them.

At every two-hundredth step the stairway, still wide and golden, curved round, and ascended again. The children were soon tired of the endless climb. They sat down to rest.

Behind them came a company of the Folk of the Mountain, chanting a strange and doleful song. Nobody liked it at all. It was horrid.

Many times the company sat down to rest. Ranni and Pilescu felt sure that the stairway led to the summit of the mountain. It was a marvellous piece of work, that stairway, beautiful all the way. Here and there, set at the sides, were glittering lamps in the shape of a rayed sun. These were so bright that the children could hardly bear to look at them.

'I think we must be going to the very top of the mountain,' said Ranni. 'It's soon sunset – and sun-worshippers usually pray to the sun at sunrise or sunset. We shall probably see them at their worship!'

Ranni was right – but he did not guess what an extra-ordinary place the summit of the mountain was!

Panting and tired, the little party climbed the last flight of steps. They came out through a great golden door into a vast corridor, with tall yellow pillars built

in two rows.

'Goodness!' said Mike, stopping in amazement. 'What a view!'

That was the first thing that struck everyone. The view from the top of the Secret Mountain was simply magnificent. All around rose other mountains, some higher, some lower, and beyond stretched the green valleys, some with a blue river winding along. It took the children's breath away, and made them feel very small indeed to look on those great mountains.

After they had feasted their eyes on the glorious scenery all around them, they turned to see what the

summit of the Secret Mountain was like. It was very strange. For one thing, it had been levelled till it was completely flat. There was an enormous wide space in the centre, floored with some kind of yellow stone that shone yellow and orange like the flight of steps up which they had come. Around this wide space, on three sides, were long pillared corridors – and on the fourth side was a great temple-like building, overlooking the steepness of the eastern side of the mountain.

The children, with Ranni and Pilescu, were taken to the great temple. The wind was very rough and cold on the top of the mountain and everyone shivered. A red-haired man came up and flung shimmering cloaks around their shoulders. These were lined with some kind of wool, and were very warm indeed.

Everyone was taken to the top of the temple, where a tall, rounded tower jutted. From this tower they could see the setting sun, falling over the rim of the western sky. As the sun disappeared, the Folk of the Secret Mountain fell on to their knees and chanted a weird song.

'A sort of prayer to the sun, I suppose,' said Ranni grimly. He spoke to Pilescu in his own language. 'I don't much like this, do you, Pilescu?'

Prince Paul pricked up his ears. 'Why don't you like it, Ranni?' he asked. Ranni would not tell him. All of them watched the sun. It disappeared suddenly over the edge of the world. At once the countryside was plunged into darkness, the valley and mountains disappeared from sight, and only the shimmering of the golden floor lighted the summit of the mountain.

A tall, red-haired man went into the centre of the shining courtyard, and spoke loudly and violently. Ranni listened and tried to understand as much as he could.

'What is he saying?' asked Mike.

'As far as I can make out he is asking the sun to stay away and let the rain come,' said Ranni. 'It seems that the rain is very much overdue, and these people are praying to the sun to dress himself in the thick clouds that will bring the rain they want. I expect they have crops somewhere on the mountainside and are in danger of losing them if the rains don't come!'

That night the little party slept on rugs in the cold, windswept temple. They were all alone on the mountain top, for their guards disappeared behind the yellow sliding door, slid it back into place again and fastened it with great long bolts. Ranni and Pilescu explored the temple, the courtyards and the corridor by the light of a torch – but there was no other door down into the mountain save the big shining one. It was as impossible to leave the top of the mountain as it had been to leave their underground room the night before.

How everyone wondered where Jack and Mafumu were, and if Captain and Mrs Arnold were anywhere near! They did not know that the four were together! When they had left the sun-trap, they had taken the passage that led inwards, and walking as quietly as they could, had come across an odd collection of store-rooms. No one was there, so they had explored them thoroughly.

In one storeroom, cut out of the solid rock, were dyes and paints of all kinds. Captain Arnold examined them closely. 'Look,' he said, 'this explains the red hair of the Folk of the Mountain. This is a very strong red dye, and these people use it for their hair, to scare any strangers they meet. And see – this is the curious yellow pigment they use for their skins!'

Everyone looked at the flat pots he was holding. They were full of the yellow ointment that the Secret Mountain Folk used on their skin! No wonder the Folk looked so very peculiar! They dyed their hair and painted their skin yellow!

When Jack knew this he no longer felt afraid of the curious appearance of the mountain people. If it was only paint and grease there was nothing strange to be afraid of! He took one of the flat pots of yellow grease and put it into his pocket. 'It will be interesting to take home!' he said cheerfully.

'If we ever *do* get home,' thought Captain Arnold to himself. They left the storerooms and went on down a curving passage that had a very high roof. Soon they heard a noise – and they came to the banks of the underground river, which swirled along through the mountain, black and swift. It was strange to see it there, running through an enormous cave.

'We shall get lost in this mountain if we are not careful,' said Captain Arnold, stopping and looking round. 'I wonder if we are getting anywhere near where this river rushed out of the mountainside, Jack.'

Jack asked Mafumu, and the boy shook his head. 'Long, long, long way,' he said mournfully. 'Mafumu not know way.'

The party of four went across the cave and left the swirling river behind. They were not sure that it was the same one that made the waterfall. Captain Arnold felt certain that the mountain held two or three rivers, that all joined to make one. It was no use to follow the one they had just left.

Soon they came to a curious door, quite round and studded with a strange pattern of suns. Behind it they heard voices! 'What are they saying, Mafumu?' whispered Jack.

Mafumu pressed himself as close to the door as he dared. His sharp ears picked up the voices – and as he listened Mafumu grew pale under his dark skin! He crept back to the others.

'They say that the sun-god is angry,' whispered Mafumu. 'They say that he is burning up the mountains because he has no servant. He needs a servant before he will hide his head in the great clouds and bring rain. And it is from one of us that he asks for a servant!'

Mafumu spoke partly in his own language and partly in Jack's. The other boy understood him and told Captain and Mrs Arnold what he had said. The Captain was silent for a long time.

'It is what I feared,' he said. 'One of us will be thrown down the mountainside to lessen the anger of their sun-god! We must try to reach Mike, Peggy, Nora and the others at all costs, as soon as we can. We must warn them!'

A Strange Journey – and a Surprise

As Captain Arnold was speaking the round door was flung open, and a tall, red-bearded man came out. It was dark in the passage, and he did not see the little company pressed against the wall. He was about to step out into the passage when there came the sound of running feet – and someone with flowing robes rushed up from the opposite direction.

There was a sharp talk, and then an excited shouting and calling. Mafumu pressed himself against Captain Arnold and whispered in his ear.

'We run quick, quick!'

Captain Arnold knew at once that their escape had been discovered, and that they must get away from there quickly. But where were they to go?

'Back to the river!' he whispered to Mrs Arnold, and the four of them made their way silently and swiftly down the passages to the dark river. Behind them they felt sure they heard the sound of voices and footsteps.

They went right to the bank of the river. 'We could get in and go across to the other side, where that high rock is, and hope that our heads wouldn't show above the water,' said Jack.

But just then Mafumu made a curious discovery. He ran to Jack, caught hold of his arm, and whispered something excitedly, pulling at Jack all the time to make him follow him. The boy went – and saw what Mafumu had so unexpectedly found. It was a small boat, of a curious shape, painted in curving stripes.

'Look! Let's get in and go down the river!' said Jack. 'I can hear someone coming now, quite plainly!'

There didn't seem anything better they could do. So they all packed themselves into the funny rounded boat and pushed off down the dark river. There were paddle-like oars in the boat, but Captain Arnold did not need to use them because the current took them along strongly.

That was a very strange journey through the heart of the Secret Mountain. Sometimes the river ran through big caves, which gleamed with green phosphorescent light. Sometimes it ran through dank tunnels, and the four in the boat could feel the slimy walls as they floated through. Once the river opened out into an enormous pool, whose sides lapped the walls of a high cave.

Mafumu was terrified. He clung to Jack tightly, and muttered strings of strange-sounding words, fingering his necklace of crocodile teeth. Jack was sorry for the other boy, especially as he felt afraid too!

The river swirled along fast. Sometimes the boat knocked against rocks and nearly upset. Once Mrs Arnold almost fell overboard, and Captain Arnold only just snatched at her in time. Everyone wondered where the journey would end.

It ended in a most astonishing manner. The river suddenly became much less violent, and the current seemed to fall away to nothing. The boat almost stopped and Captain Arnold had to use the paddles to get it forward. They were in a fairly wide tunnel with a low roof, and not far ahead there seemed to be an archway, through which a bright light shone.

'We're arriving somewhere,' said Captain Arnold. 'Well, we can't go back, so we must go forward! I wonder what that bright light is!'

They soon found out! The boat went slowly forward, passed through the archway – and the four found, to their enormous amazement, that the river flowed through what looked like a big and most magnificent room!

The floor was of great smooth stones, polished till they shone. The walls were covered with brilliant hangings, all the colours of the rainbow, and the ceiling which was domed in glittering stones, rose up high and beautiful. From it hung the great gleaming lamp that gave the bright light the four had seen through the archway.

Stone tables stood here and there, and there were piles of soft rugs on the floor. Great vases and pitchers stood about filled with the brilliant flowers of the countryside. Three parrots screeched in a golden cage and five little monkeys huddled together in a corner.

Through the middle of this strange apartment, hidden right in the heart of the mountain, flowed one of the many underground rivers that gurgled their way towards the openings in the mountain rock through which they could fall down the hillside.

'This reminds me of a fairy-tale!' said Mrs Arnold in the greatest amazement. 'What are we going to do? Get out and explore this extraordinary place? It's like a palace or something, built underground!'

No one was in the enormous, beautiful room except

the parrots and the monkeys. Captain Arnold wondered whether or not to let his little party get out of the boat, which was still flowing gently along. And then he caught sight of something just ahead of him on the river.

It was a great golden gate stretched across the water! How strange! The boat would certainly be able to get no further, unless they could open the gate. Captain Arnold had a strange feeling that it would be better not to land in the strange room, but to go on, and see if by chance he could open the gate and go on his way.

So the boat went on towards the shining gate – and that was the end of their strange journey! For sitting along the banks of the river beside the gate were about a dozen of the red-haired Folk of the Mountain! As soon as they saw the boat coming they leapt to their feet in amazement and shouted and pointed!

The boat came to a stop by the gate. 'It's all up now,' said Captain Arnold in disgust. 'We can't escape any further! They've got us!'

Sure enough, they were prisoners in about half a minute! The boat was pulled to the bank, and the Mountain Folk dragged the little company from their boat. They seemed astonished to see Jack and Mafumu.

'They don't know that Jack and Mafumu are here, of course,' said Captain Arnold. 'They know *we've* escaped because our cave is empty, but they didn't know anything about these two boys! Look – they are taking us back to that strange and beautiful room.'

They passed through a great doorway into the big apartment they had just floated through. But now it was no longer empty! On a kind of throne at one end sat a tall, red-bearded, yellow-skinned man, whose eyes glinted strangely as he gazed down at the four people before him.

'He must be their chief or king,' said Captain Arnold. 'I don't like the look of him much.'

Behind the chief stood a company of the Mountain Folk, all with flaming red beards. They held curious spears that glittered from end to end, and from their heads rose shining sun-rays that gleamed as they turned to one another. Mafumu was so frightened that he could hardly stand and Jack had to hold him up.

The big chief spoke in a harsh and stony voice. Only Mafumu understood a little of what he said, and what he heard made him tremble, for he knew that these sun-worshippers meant to throw one or more of them down the mountainside as a kind of sacrifice to the sun. The red-bearded chief gave a sharp order, and at once the men with spears closed round the four and completely surrounded them.

They were marched off through the great room, with the screeching of the three parrots sounding in their ears. And they were taken to the top of the mountain, where the rest of the party were! But the way they went was quite different from the way that the others had taken!

They were marched to a small room in which stood what looked like a cage of gold, beautifully carved and worked. 'Look!' said Jack, pointing upwards. 'There's a hole going through the roof of this room, up and up and up!'

There was – and it was there for a curious purpose, too. It was to take the cage upwards, just as a lift shaft holds a rising lift. The golden cage was a kind of simple lift – but the ropes that hauled it up were pulled by men and not by machinery.

The little party were crammed into the cage, with four of the Mountain Folk. The door was shut. One of the men shouted a sharp order – and immediately twenty men began to haul strongly on some massive ropes that hung down from another hole in the roof.

The cage shot upwards like a lift! Mafumu was terrified, he had never even been in a lift before! The others were amazed, but they showed no fear, and Mrs Arnold bent down to comfort the poor little boy.

Up and up they went, sometimes fast, sometimes slow, right to the very top of the mountain. They came to a stop underneath a round and gleaming trapdoor, which was bolted underneath. One of the men slid back the bolts, pressed a spring and the door opened upwards, falling back silently on its hinges. The cage rose slowly once again, and when it was level with the ground it stopped.

The door of the golden cage was opened, and everyone stepped out. Captain and Mrs Arnold looked round. They had no idea where they were at first – and then they realised that they were on the very summit of the Secret Mountain! They held their breath as they looked at the magnificent view!

The cage-lift had come up through a hole right in the very middle of the vast courtyard that spread over the top of the mountain. Jack took a quick look round and wondered if any of the others were there, but he could see no one.

They *were* there, of course! They were in the temple,

eating some of the fruit that had been brought to them, having wrapped themselves up well in the rugs, for the wind that blew across the mountain at that time of year was strong and cold, despite the hot sun.

It was Prince Paul who saw the strange and surprising sight of the cage-lift coming up in the middle of the courtyard! He was looking out through the open doorway of the temple, and to his very great amazement he saw what seemed to be a big trapdoor slowly open and bend itself back. He swallowed his mouthful in surprise, and choked. Mike banged him on the back.

'Don't! Don't! Look! Look!' choked poor Paul, trying to point through the doorway. But everyone thought he was upset because he was choking, and Peggy took a turn at banging him between the shoulders.

Paul saw the golden cage rise up through the trapdoor opening. He saw Captain and Mrs Arnold, Jack and Mafumu get out, with their four guards, and his eyes nearly fell out of his head with amazement and delight. He went quite purple in the face, and leapt to his feet.

'Look!' he yelled to the others. And at last they looked. When they saw the unexpected appearance of eight people in the middle of the smooth courtyard, and when Mike, Peggy and Nora saw that two of them were their own father and mother, what an excitement there was!

With shouts and shrieks the children rushed down the temple steps and ran towards the little company in the courtyard. In half a minute they were hugging their father and mother, exclaiming over them, thumping Jack on the back, shouting a hundred questions, and

hugging little Mafumu, who was quite overjoyed at seeing all his lost friends so suddenly again.

'This is a surprise! This is a surprise!' everyone kept saying. And, indeed, it was!

The Escape of Ranni and Pilescu

When everyone had calmed down a little, they looked round to see what had become of the four guards who had come up in the cage-lift with Jack and the others. But they were gone! They had silently stepped into the golden cage once more, and had disappeared from sight into the heart of the mountain!

Captain Arnold ran to where the trapdoor lay smoothly in the floor of the courtyard. He tried to get his fingers between the edges of the door and the stone of the courtyard – but they fitted so exactly that it was impossible.

'In any case it will be locked and bolted the other side,' he said. 'There's no way of escape there. How did you get here, Mike? Through this trapdoor?'

Mike told him about the enormous flights of shining steps that led up to the golden door. He showed the newcomers the door itself, but no matter how they tried they could not slide it back.

The children were all so excited at seeing their father and mother again, and at having Jack and Mafumu once more, that they forgot their worries and chatted happily, telling one another their adventures. Only the grown-ups looked grave, and talked solemnly together, apart from the children.

'Somehow we must think of a way to escape,' said Pilescu. 'These Folk of the Secret Mountain are savage and ignorant. They think that the sun is angry with them, and they want to give him a servant to make their peace with him. Which of us will be chosen for that? I don't like to think.'

'None of us is safe,' said Captain Arnold. 'Is it possible to lie in wait for the guards who come to give you food, Pilescu, overpower them, and escape down the golden stair?'

'We could try,' said Ranni doubtfully. 'But I fear it would be no use. Still, it seems the only thing to do.'

At that moment Jack came up. He had been showing the other children the pot of strange yellow paint that he had taken from the storeroom among the caves in the mountain. He looked very peculiar because he had tried out some of the paint on his own face, and his skin was now as bright yellow as the Folk of the Mountain!

Ranni and Pilescu, who did not know about the pigment, stared at him in horror.

'Jack! What is the matter with you?' cried Pilescu. 'Are you ill?'

'Very!' grinned Jack. 'I think I must have got yellow fever, Pilescu! Have you got any medicine to make me better?'

The other children crowded round, giggling and laughing, and Pilescu knew it was a joke. He looked closely at Jack.

'You have got yellow paint on your face,' he said. 'You look like one of the Folk of the Mountain!'

'And you, Pilescu, would look *exactly* like one if you

painted *your* face,' said Jack, 'because you have a flaming red beard as they have. But yours is a real red beard, not a dyed one!'

No sooner had Jack said these words than the same thought flashed into Pilescu's head and Captain Arnold's at the same moment. Pilescu snatched the pot of pigment from Jack and looked at it. He dipped his finger into it and rubbed it over the back of his hand. At once his skin gleamed the same yellow as the skin of the Mountain Folk.

'I've thought the same thing as you, Pilescu,' said Captain Arnold, in excitement. 'If you used this paint you would pass for one of the Secret Mountain people! You and Ranni both have the bright red hair and beards of Baronian men – if you paint your skin yellow, you will look very like the Folk of the Mountain – and maybe our way of escape lies through you!'

Immediately all was excitement. Everyone talked at once. Everyone thought it was a simply marvellous idea. In the end Captain Arnold silenced the party and spoke seriously to them all.

'We must lose no further time in talk,' he said. 'I propose that both Ranni and Pilescu paint their faces with this yellow pigment and try to escape with the guards when they come. If only they can find their way back to where our planes are, they may be able to find some way of rescuing us all. It's the only chance that I can see.'

'There are some robes in the temple with the rugs!' cried Mike. 'I tried them on this morning. They would fit Ranni and Pilescu. Come and try them!'

141

In the greatest excitement the little company went to the temple. Ranni and Pilescu tried on the coloured robes and they fitted well enough. The flowing garments looked strange on the two big men, and everyone laughed.

Captain Arnold carefully rubbed the curious yellow pigment into the skin of the Baronians' faces, necks and hands. With the flowing robes, yellow skin and flaming beards they looked exactly like the Folk of the Secret Mountain! Poor Mafumu, unused to extraordinary happenings of this sort, could hardly believe that it was still Ranni and Pilescu, and he shrank away from them in fear.

'It is getting near the time when sun-worshippers come to pray to the sun at sunset,' said Captain Arnold looking over the mountains to where the sun was swinging down towards the edge of the world. 'Maybe many of the Mountain Folk will come, and then you can mix with them easily enough when they go!'

It was decided that Ranni and Pilescu should hide behind two great pillars near the sliding door. If they were not discovered they could mix with the Mountain Folk as they went down the stairs again, and might escape unseen in that way.

The sun swung lower – and suddenly, from behind the great golden door came the sound of chanting. It was the Mountain Folk coming to sing their prayers to the sun! The door slid to one side, and up the shining stairway came scores of the curious Folk, their beards gleaming red in the setting sun.

The leader went to the tower of the temple. All the

rest spread themselves out on the flat courtyard, and flung themselves down on their faces when the man in the temple sounded a loud and echoing bell. They chanted a sad and doleful dirge for about ten minutes, whilst Captain Arnold and the rest looked on.

Behind the big pillars Ranni and Pilescu waited their chance. As soon as the sun disappeared over the edge of the world and darkness fell on the mountain the people stood up and ranged themselves in lines. Then still singing, led by their tall leader, they made their way back to the stairway that led down into the dark mountain.

And, slipping to the end of the lines, went two red-bearded folk that did not belong to the mountain! Ranni and Pilescu joined the company, and tried to do exactly as the men in front did. They passed through the shining doorway and down the golden stairs. The door slid back silently into place – and Ranni and Pilescu were gone from sight!

'They've gone!' said Jack, slipping his hand through Mike's arm. 'They've gone! Oh, I do wonder how they'll get on. I do hope they won't be caught!'

No one came to disturb them again that evening. The little party went into the temple and tried to find the most sheltered corner. The mountain wind blew without stopping, day and night, and it was difficult to find anywhere that was not full of draughts. The girls cuddled up to Mrs Arnold, and the boys and Captain Arnold found a bigger corner and piled rugs over themselves.

They all slept soundly that night, in spite of the cold.

Captain and Mrs Arnold were glad to be with their children again, and hoped against hope that somehow Ranni and Pilescu would find a way to escape from the mountain and bring help to the prisoners.

For two days nothing happened. The Folk of the Mountain came up once at sunrise and once at sunset to chant their strange songs and prayers. Guards came to bring food and water. Curiously enough they did not miss Ranni and Pilescu at all – partly because Captain Arnold had told the party to split up, and be in various places on the summit of the mountain, instead of all together.

'Then when our guards come, they will not be able to count us up, because we shall be all over the place!' said Captain Arnold. 'And unless they actually go to look for everyone they will not guess that two of our party are missing!'

But the guards did not think for one minute that anyone *could* be missing! After all, no one could escape down the trapdoor for it was bolted underneath – and no one, so they thought, could escape down the golden stairway without being seen. So the little party lived peacefully for two days, with no excitements at all.

Then things began to happen. The golden cage once more came up through the trapdoor in the centre of the vast courtyard! Mrs Arnold happened to be standing nearby and she had a great surprise when she saw the trapdoor suddenly rise up and the golden cage appear. She ran to tell the others. They came to watch who was coming.

The chief himself walked from the golden lift! He

was very tall, and very thin. His beard flamed in the sun, and his clothes swung round him like shimmering water as he walked. His yellow skin was wrinkled and drawn. He was an old, old man, but powerful and with piercing, eagle-like eyes.

He gave a sharp order. Men stepped out from the cage and came behind him. He walked solemnly to the temple, where he chanted several prayers to the sun in a strong harsh voice. Then he turned to his servants who rounded up the little company of prisoners, and brought them before the chief. He ran his strange eyes over them and then looked at his servants in surprise. It was quite plain that he thought someone was missing!

He asked a sharp question. The servants hurriedly counted the prisoners and then sent two of their number to search the summit of the mountain thoroughly.

'They've gone to find Ranni and Pilescu,' whispered Jack. 'Well, they won't find them here!'

And they didn't, of course, though they hunted in every corner and cranny. Ranni and Pilescu had disappeared completely.

The chief was angry. His eyes flamed, and his mouth became hard and straight. He addressed his servants fiercely, and they flung themselves on their faces before him. No one but Mafumu could understand what he was saying, and even Mafumu could not understand everything!

The chief walked majestically over to the company of prisoners and looked into each one's face. No one flinched except poor Mafumu, who was in a state of real terror, partly because he was afraid of the yellow-skinned chief and partly because he knew something that the others didn't know!

The chief was choosing who was to be the servant of the sun! He glared into Jack's face. He stared closely at poor Nora and Peggy. He took Paul's chin in his hand and peered at him. Nobody liked it at all.

Mafumu was very sad. Whom would the chief choose? Somebody must be the sacrifice to the sun. And poor Mafumu would have to break the news, for no one else understood what the yellow-skinned chief was doing!

The Servant of the Sun

The tall chief took hold of the little prince and called out some strange words to his followers. At once two men stepped forward and took the frightened boy. He did not know what they were going to do with him, but he was determined not to show that he was afraid.

So, rather white, he stood up proudly and looked the chief straight in the face. Mike and the others felt proud of him.

Paul was marched off alone He was taken to the golden door, which slid back silently. Then he disappeared down the stairway, and the door once more shut like magic. Captain Arnold stepped forward angrily.

'What are you going to do to the boy?' he cried. 'Bring him back!'

The chief laughed, then turned on his heel. He went up to the tower of the temple and began what seemed like a long prayer to the sun.

It was left to poor trembling Mafumu to break the news to the others. In his few English words he tried to explain that little Paul was to be the servant of the sun. Everyone listened in amazement and horror. Captain and Mrs Arnold who had feared that something like this could happen ever since they had been brought to the temple on top of the mountain, looked despairingly at one another.

'I can't see how we can possibly save him,' said Captain Arnold at last. They all sat down in the shade, and Peggy and Nora began to cry. If even grown-up people couldn't do anything, then things were indeed in a bad way!

Mike and Jack and Mafumu talked together. Jack would never give up hope. He was that kind of boy. But Mike was full of dismay, and as for Mafumu, he was simply shivering with worry and fright. He kept as close to Jack as he could, as if he thought that Jack would protect him from everything.

Jack was very edgy, though he didn't show it. 'I wish you'd do something instead of shivering all over me,' he said to Mafumu, pushing the boy away.

'Give him a pencil or a notebook to play with,' said Mike. 'He's only a little kid, and you can't blame him for being a bit scared.'

Jack put his hand into his pocket and brought out a diary. He had been keeping the tale of their adventures there, day by day. He handed it to Mafumu.

'Here you are. Play with this over in the corner there,' he said. Mafumu took the notebook eagerly. He turned over each page one by one, rubbing his fingers over the pages in which Jack had written. He could not understand anything, of course, because he could not write or read.

He came to where Jack had written the day before. After that the pages were blank. Mafumu was puzzled. Why was nothing written in one half of the book? He rolled himself over beside Jack and pointed to the blank pages.

Jack tried to explain to Mafumu. 'Today I write, tomorrow I write, but not till the day has gone,' he said.

'Jack, what's the date today?' asked Mike idly. 'I've really lost count of the days, you know! I don't know if it's Sunday, Monday, Tuesday, or what – or if it's the tenth, eleventh, twenty-first, or thirtieth of the month!'

'Well, I can tell you, because I've written down our adventures every day,' said Jack. 'It's Wednesday – and it's the sixteenth. Look.'

Mike took the diary. He glanced at the next day, and gave an exclamation.

'Oh, Jack! Look what it says for tomorrow!'

'What?' asked Jack, surprised.

'It says there will be an eclipse of the sun,' said Mike. 'I do wonder if we'll see it here?'

'Let's ask your father,' said Jack. So the two boys went across to Captain Arnold, with the faithful Mafumu following at their heels.

'Dad! It says in Jack's diary that there is an eclipse of the sun tomorrow!' said Mike. 'Do you think there is any chance at all of seeing it here?'

'What's an eclipse of the sun?' asked Peggy. 'I know we've learnt about it in school, but I've quite forgotten what happens.'

'It's quite simple,' said Mike. 'All that happens is that the moon on its way through the sky passes in front of the sun, and blocks out the sun's light for a little while. It eclipses the sun's light, and for a time the world looks strange and rather eerie because there is no sunlight in the daytime!'

Captain Arnold sprang to his feet. To Mike's enormous surprise he snatched Jack's diary from him and looked at what was printed there in the space for the next day.

'Eclipse of the sun, 11.43 a.m.,' he read. 'Is this this year's diary? Yes! My word! Eclipse of the sun *tomorrow*! It's unbelievable!'

He spoke in such an excited voice that everyone came round him at once.

'What's the matter? Why are you so excited?' cried Mike. Only Mrs Arnold guessed. Her eyes were bright and hopeful.

'I'll tell you. Listen carefully,' said Captain Arnold. He lowered his voice, for although he did not think that any of the Mountain Folk were listening anywhere, or could understand a word he said, he was not taking any chances.

'Mike has told you what an eclipse of the sun means. It means that the moon passes exactly in front of the sun, and it only happens rarely. If we were in England the sun would not be completely hidden by the moon – but here in Africa it will, and the whole countryside will become as dark as night!'

The children listened in excitement. What a strange happening it would be!

'Now these Mountain Folk are sun-worshippers,' said Captain Arnold. 'It is quite plain that they have the custom of throwing unfortunate people over the mountainside to sacrifice to the sun, when they want to please him, or ask him to grant a prayer. I am afraid that our little Paul has been chosen, and will be beyond our

151

help tomorrow unless we do something. And now I see what we can do!'

'What?' cried everyone.

'Well, we will get Mafumu to explain to these people, when they next come up here, that I will kill the sun tomorrow, unless they set Paul free!' said Captain Arnold.

'How do you mean – kill the sun?' asked Nora in wonder.

'Well, to them, when the eclipse happens, it will seem as if the sun is being killed!' said Captain Arnold, smiling. 'They won't know that it is only the moon passing in front of the sun that is blocking out the light – they will really think I have done something to the sun they worship!'

'Oh, Captain Arnold – it sounds too good to be true!' cried Jack. 'Won't they be amazed? I wonder if they will set us all free if we do this.'

'Probably,' said Captain Arnold. 'We can do our best, anyway. Now, I wonder if the Mountain Folk will come up at sunset tonight, and sing their mournful prayers!'

But, to everyone's great disappointment, not a single person came. No word was heard of the little Prince. Nothing happened at all. Captain and Mrs Arnold felt uneasy about Paul, but they did not tell the others.

'Probably there is a great hunt going on in the mountain for Ranni and Pilescu!' said Captain Arnold. 'I do wonder what has happened to them. If only they have managed to slip out of the rock entrance, and find help somewhere.'

The night passed. It was cold up on the mountain

top and everyone slept as usual muffled up in the soft warm rugs. The children missed Prince Paul and were sad when they thought of him. They knew he must be feeling very lonely and frightened all by himself, no matter how brave a face he put on when the Mountain Folk were there.

The dawn came, and the whole sky around was full of dancing silvery light.

'You can see such an enormous lot of sky from the top of a mountain,' said Mike, gazing all round. 'Look – there comes the sun!'

The golden sun rose slowly into the sky and the children watched it. It was so beautiful that each child was filled with awe.

'It's certainly the king of the sky!' said Mike. 'I really am not surprised that these strange wild tribes worship the sun! Oh dear – I do miss Paul. I wonder where he is.'

They soon saw him again. Mike spied the trapdoor slowly open in the middle of the big courtyard, and he called out to the others.

'Someone's coming. Look!'

They all looked. The golden cage rose slowly through the space left by the trapdoor, and in it the children could see the tall chief with his flaming red beard, two servants – and a small figure dressed in the most wonderful shimmering robes they had ever seen.

'Why – it's Paul dressed like that!' cried Mike in amazement. 'And look what he's got on his head!'

Paul was certainly dressed in a very strange manner. He wore the shimmering golden garments down to his

feet, and the flowing sleeves even covered his hands. On his head was a great headdress made in the likeness of a glittering sun, with golden rays springing upwards.

The boy looked magnificent, and he walked very proudly. He had guessed that he was to be the servant of the sun, and he was afraid – but he was going to show Mike and the others that he was brave and courageous. He walked behind the chief, and sent a cheerful though rather quivery smile at his friends.

'Dear Paul. Good little Paul,' said Nora.

'I do feel proud of him,' said Mike, with a funny little break in his voice.

And then Captain Arnold stepped forward and shouted

in such a tremendous voice that everyone jumped.

'*Stop*! I command you to *stop*!'

The tall chief stopped in his walk and glared round at Captain Arnold. He did not understand the words that the captain said – but he understood their meaning. There was no mistaking that at all!

'Come here Mafumu,' commanded Captain Arnold. The little boy came to him, trembling. 'Tell the chief that I will kill the sun if he does anything to Paul,' said the Captain. Mafumu did not understand, so Jack explained as best he could in simple words.

Mafumu nodded. He knelt down before the chief, and banged his forehead on the ground before him.

Mafumu cried out some strange words to the chief, and then banged his forehead on the ground again. The chief frowned and looked at Captain Arnold. He said something sharp to Mafumu.

'Chief say no, Captain will not kill sun,' said the little

155

boy. 'He say that when the sun is high, high, high, Paul will go to the sun.'

'When the sun is high,' repeated Captain Arnold. 'That means noon – twelve o'clock – and the eclipse is due at about a quarter to. Well – that will just about do it! Tell the chief I *will* kill the sun unless he sets us all free, Mafumu.'

But the chief laughed in their faces. He set off towards the tower of the temple, Paul following behind in his shimmering robes. Everyone watched them go – and how the children hoped that the eclipse of the sun would actually happen. It seemed too strange a thing to be really true.

The Sun Disappears!

The little company of prisoners was not allowed to go into the temple that morning. The two servants stood at the door and prevented anyone from entering. Mike could see the figure of Paul up on the tower with the tall chief, who was muttering and chanting all kinds of weird words to the sun. Paul waved to Mike once, and Mike waved back.

'It's all right, Paul. You needn't be afraid,' shouted Mike. 'We're going to save you!'

But the wind took away his words and Paul did not hear. He stood there bravely, the wonderful headdress he was wearing shining and glinting in the sun.

As the sun rose higher and the day grew hotter, Captain Arnold and the rest of his party found what shade they could. There was always a big wind blowing on the summit of the high mountain, but even so the rays of the sun as it rose high were flaming hot.

At about eleven o'clock the great golden door slid open, and an enormous company of Mountain Folk came singing up the shining stairway. They were dressed in shimmering robes rather like Paul's, and looked marvellous as they trooped out on to the great courtyard. Their faces were yellower than ever, and the men's beards had been freshly dyed and flamed like fire.

They ranged themselves over the courtyard and then began to dance a strange dance. Their feet stamped, their robes swung and shimmered, their voices rose and fell in a peculiar chant.

'A sort of sun dance,' said Captain Arnold. Everyone was worried and anxious, but they could not help marvelling as they watched the curious sun-worshippers performing their extraordinary dance.

Captain Arnold glanced at his watch. It was half-past eleven. He looked anxiously up at the sun, which was almost at its highest point. No moon could be seen, of course, for the sun was so bright. But it was there all right, travelling through the sky.

An enormous gong boomed out from the temple. One of the servants of the chief was sounding it. The children had seen it there, but there had been nothing to bang it with – and now it was sounding over the mountain top, booming its great solemn note all around. The valleys below took up the note and threw it back – and soon, from everywhere around, the echoes came back until it seemed as if the whole earth and sky were filled with the booming of the gong.

At once all the sun-worshippers fell on their knees. The chief waited until the sound of the gong had died away and then he spoke in a loud voice. He brought Prince Paul forward, and the boy stood there on the temple tower, his robes blowing and shining in the wind.

'Captain Arnold, will the eclipse start soon?' asked Jack nervously. He was terribly afraid that something would happen to Paul before they could prevent it.

Captain Arnold glanced at his watch.

'It will begin in two minutes,' he said. 'Now, *I* am going to take a hand in this game! Watch me!'

He ran with quick, light steps to the tower. The servants at the entrance were taken by surprise, and he slipped through easily. He raced up the stone steps and in a moment or two was standing beside the chief and Paul.

And then things began to happen! Captain Arnold turned to the great sun and shook his fist at it. He shouted at it! He snatched a knife from his belt and threw it high into the air at the sun! The knife made a great curve in the air and disappeared over the mountainside!

'He kills the sun, he kills the sun!' shouted Mafumu, who suddenly understood what Captain Arnold was pretending to do. The Mountain Folk understood Mafumu's shout and rose to their feet in alarm and confusion. The servants of the chief ran to capture Captain Arnold – and then a strange thing happened.

A tiny piece seemed suddenly to be bitten out of the sun! A small black shadow appeared at one side! The moon was beginning to pass in front of it, and was hiding a very small piece.

Mafumu saw it and was astonished. He pointed at the sun, and shouted in alarm. 'The sun is being eaten! See, see!'

A great silence fell on the mountain top. Everyone was watching the sun in the sky, covering their faces with their hands, and looking through their fingers to avoid the brilliance. The servants who had come to capture Captain Arnold watched, too, trembling.

The moon passed further in front of the sun and a

bigger piece became completely dark. A moan of fear came from the watching Mountain Folk. They did not understand what an eclipse of the sun was, and they really thought that their precious sun was being killed!

Not one of them guessed that it was merely the moon passing in front of the sun and blocking out its light for a while. They fell on their faces and muttered all kinds of strange prayers. And when they looked up again they saw that half of the sun was gone!

And now the world began to look weird and unearthly. The sunlight dwindled and died. A strange half-light came over the whole countryside. Birds stopped singing. The monkeys in the trees huddled together, frightened. The frogs thought that night was coming and began to croak.

The children were afraid too, although they knew quite well that it was only an eclipse they were watching. They had never seen one before, and this was a complete eclipse, with every bit of daylight and sunlight gradually going from the world they looked upon. As for poor Mafumu he had never in his life been so frightened. He crouched on the ground shivering like a jelly, and Jack did his best to comfort him.

The chief up on the tower was watching the dying sun with fear and amazement. He too was trembling. Could it be that this man was really killing their wonderful sun-god who shone so brightly in the sky each day? He could not understand it. He threw out his arms to the sun, and shouted to it, trying to comfort the failing sun, and to make it shine brightly again! Captain Arnold folded his arms, looked very stern, and it really seemed for all the world as if he were the conjurer who had worked the trick!

And now even stranger things happened! The sky became as black as night and the stars came out. They shone brilliantly, and starlight lighted the earth instead of sunlight.

'Don't be afraid,' Mrs Arnold said to the scared children, who had not expected this. 'The sun is gone now, lost behind the moon – so, of course, it is like night-time, and the stars shine out. You must remember that the stars are always in the sky, all through the day – but we don't see them because daylight is so bright. But now that the daylight has gone, we can see the stars shining.'

It all seemed simple enough when Mrs Arnold explained it – but the terrified Mountain Folk had no idea of what was really happening, and they were quite mad with fear and terror. They shouted and moaned, and beat their foreheads and dropped to their knees.

Up on the tower it was quite dark. Captain Arnold caught hold of the astonished little prince and whispered in his ear.

'Go down the stone steps and join the others, Paul. No one will stop you now. You are safe.'

Paul made his way to the steps and went down them thankfully. He felt his way to the children, and clasped Mike's hand in joy. Mike put his arms round him, and the others clustered round Paul, who felt strange in his flowing garments.

'The eclipse came just at the right moment to save you, Paul, old boy,' said Jack in his ear. 'You're safe now.

You *were* brave. We were awfully proud of you.'

Paul's heart glowed. He had often been laughed at because he was rather a baby – and now he felt a hero! He kept close to the children and watched the rest of the eclipse.

As soon as Captain Arnold saw that the sun was completely gone, he began to shout, pretending that he was threatening the lost sun. The chief went down on his knees and begged for mercy, quite certain that Captain Arnold was the most powerful magician in the whole world!

Then gradually the moon passed right across the sun, and a little bit of one side began to show again. The stars slowly disappeared as the moon passed from the sun, and the strange half-light appeared once more. This was too much for the Mountain Folk. It was bad enough to have seen the sun die, as they thought – but now something else was happening, and they could not bear it.

Shouting and groaning, they rushed to the golden stairway and poured down it, slipping and falling as they went. The two servants who had been on the tower went too, deserting their chief in their fear. He was left on the tower, kneeling down before Captain Arnold.

Gradually the sun became itself again as the moon passed right across it, and the black shadow fled. The glorious daylight flooded the mountains, and the golden sun poured its rays down once more. Birds sang again. The monkeys chattered in delight. The brief and unexpected night was gone, and the world was itself again.

Captain Arnold took the frightened chief by the shoulder and led him firmly down the steps. He called to Mafumu.

'Mafumu, tell the chief he must let us all go now, or I will kill his sun again,' commanded the Captain. Mafumu understood. He was feeling better now that the sun had come back, and he thought that Captain Arnold must be the most powerful man in all the world. No matter how often the others explained what had really happened, Mafumu would never, never believe anything but that Captain Arnold had done something to the sun!

Mafumu, feeling important and grand, said something to the chief. The man was angry that such a small boy should speak in that way to him, and he took no notice at all. He strode away from Captain Arnold and went towards the trapdoor, which was still lying open, flat on the ground. The golden cage was there awaiting him.

'Mafumu, tell him that we are going down the golden stairway, and that his servants must let us out of the rock entrance,' said Captain Arnold. Mafumu shouted at the chief. The man nodded, and entered the cage. In a flash he was gone, and the trapdoor still lay flat on the ground, for he had not troubled to bolt it.

'Well, *he's* gone, and so has everyone else,' said Mike, with a laugh. 'My word – what an adventure! I don't mind saying that I felt very odd myself when the sun began to disappear and the stars shone out. I could do with something to eat. Let's go and get some of those flat cakes from the temple before we go down the stairs.'

'Well, hurry then,' said Captain Arnold. 'I want to go

whilst the going is good!'

The boys ran to get the cakes and some fruit. They brought it out in the flat dishes, and joined Captain and Mrs Arnold and the girls, who were walking towards the golden door.

But as they came near, the door began to slide silently shut! Captain Arnold gave a shout and ran towards it.

'Hurry! They are shutting us out!'

He got there just as the door completely closed. There it rose above him, a tall, shining door, as wide as a great gate – fast shut.

'They've tricked us!' shouted the Captain angrily, and he hammered on the door. But there was no handle, no latch, nothing to get hold of or to loosen. There was no getting through that enormous door it was plain!

Big, Big Bird That Sings R-r-r-r-r!

'The trapdoor!' shouted Mike. 'We can escape through that. The chief has left it open!'

The boys ran helter-skelter across the vast courtyard to where the opening was. They were half-afraid that the trapdoor would close before they got there. But it didn't.

The four boys stood by the lift-opening and looked down. The lift-shaft ran straight down below their feet, cut out of solid rock. The golden cage was not to be seen, of course. The opening looked dark and narrow as it disappeared into the darkness of the heart of the mountain.

'I don't see how we could escape down there,' said Mike. 'We would need a tremendous long rope to begin with – which we haven't got – and also, just suppose the lift came up as we went down!'

'That golden cage was pulled up and down by ropes, wasn't it?' said Mrs Arnold. 'Well, surely those must still be running down one side of the opening.'

'Of course they must,' said Captain Arnold. 'We'll look for those.'

But the ropes that sent the lift up and down had been cut! Captain Arnold found them easily enough, running in a cleverly cut groove at one side of the lift-opening.

But when he pulled at them they came up in his hand, not more than ten feet long! Somehow they had been cut and were of no use at all!

'We may as well shut the trapdoor,' said Captain Arnold, in disgust and disappointment. 'It is dangerous to leave it open in case one of you goes and tumbles down the hole. Well – we really are in a fix now!'

'How all the Mountain Folk must be laughing at us!' said

Mike. 'We are nicely caught! Can't get down, and can't get up – here we are stuck on the top of a mountain for the rest of our lives!'

Captain Arnold did not like the look of things at all. He was afraid that the Folk of the Secret Mountain would open the sliding door and spring on them during the night. But he said this only to Mrs Arnold, for he did not want to frighten the children.

'Well, we've all had a great deal of excitement today,' he said. 'Let's go into the cool temple, have a good meal, and a rest.'

So into the temple they went, and were soon munching away at the flat cakes and the sweet juicy fruit. Then the children and Mrs Arnold settled themselves down for a rest whilst Captain Arnold kept watch. It was arranged that either the Captain, Jack or Mike should keep guard, so that at any rate the little party would not be taken unawares.

The night came as suddenly as usual. The stars flashed out brightly, and the world of mountains lay peacefully under the beautiful starlight. Captain Arnold went to examine the trapdoor to make sure that no one could come upon them from there, and then he went to look at the sliding door. But it was still fast shut and there seemed to be no sound from the other side at all.

The night passed peacefully. First the Captain kept watch and then the two boys. But nothing happened. The dawn came, and the sun rose. The children awoke and stretched themselves. They were hungry – but, alas, except for a few of the flat cakes, there was no food left at all.

'I hope they are not going to starve us out,' said Mike hungrily, as Captain Arnold shared out the few cakes between the party. 'I shouldn't like that at all.'

'This adventure is exciting, but awfully uncomfortable,' said Nora.

At about ten o'clock the great golden door slid back again. Up the stairs came the Folk of the Mountain – but this time they carried shining spears! They were on the warpath, that was plain!

Captain Arnold had half-expected this. He made the children go into a corner, and he went to meet the tall chief, with Mafumu close beside him to talk for him.

But the chief was in no mood for talking. He too carried a spear, and he looked very fiercely at Captain Arnold.

'Tell him I will kill his sun again, Mafumu,' said the Captain desperately.

'Chief say he kill you first,' said poor Mafumu, his teeth chattering. And, indeed, it certainly looked as if this was what the chief meant to do, for he lowered his spear and pointed it threateningly at Captain Arnold.

The Captain had a revolver. He did not want to shoot the chief, but thought he might as well frighten him. He drew his revolver and fired it into the air. The noise of the shot echoed round the mountains in a most terrifying manner. The chief jumped with fright. All the Mountain Folk began to jabber and shout.

But one, cleverer than the others, aimed his spear at Captain Arnold. The shining weapon flew through the air, struck the gun in the Captain's hand, and sent it flying to ground with a clang. None of the Mountain Folk dared to pick it up, and Captain Arnold did not dare to either – for a different reason! He was not afraid of the revolver – but he was afraid of the spears around him!

The chief shouted out a harsh order, and twelve men ran up with spears. They took hold of all the little company, and before ten minutes had gone by, each grown-up and child was bound with thin, strong ropes!

'What will they do with us?' said Nora, who was very angry because her wrists had been bound too tightly.

Nobody knew. But it was plain that the little party were to be taken below into the heart of the mountain. They were not to be left on the summit.

'I expect the chief is afraid we will do something to his beloved sun if he leaves us up here,' said Jack. 'I wish another eclipse would happen! What a shock it would give them all!'

The chief gave orders for the captives to be taken down the shining stairway – but just as they were about to go, there came a most extraordinary noise!

At first it was far away and quiet – a little humming – but soon it grew louder and louder, and the mountainside echoed with the sound of throbbing.

'R-r-r-r-r-r!' went the noise. 'R-r-r-r-r-r! R-r-r-r-r-r-r!'

The Folk of the Secret Mountain stopped and listened, their eyes wide with amazement. This was a strange noise. What could it be?

The children were puzzled at first too – but almost at once Jack knew what the noise was, and he lifted up his voice in a shout.

'It's an aeroplane! An aeroplane! Can't you hear it? It's coming nearer!'

Captain Arnold was amazed. He knew that it was the noise made by the throbbing of aeroplane engines – but what aeroplane? Surely – surely – it could not be the White Swallow?

The noise came nearer – and then a black speck could be seen flying towards the mountainside. It really was an aeroplane – no doubt about that at all!

The Mountain Folk saw it too. They cried out in surprise and pointed to it. 'What are they saying, Mafumu?' shouted Jack.

'They say, "Big, big bird, big, big bird that sings r-r-r-r-r-r-r!"' said Mafumu, his eyes shining and his teeth flashing. The children laughed, excited and eager. Something was going to happen – they were sure of it!

The aeroplane came nearer and nearer, growing bigger as it came. 'It *is* the White Swallow!' shouted Captain Arnold. 'I'd know the sound of her engines anywhere, the beauty! Ranni and Pilescu must have somehow got back to the planes, made the White Swallow ready for taking off – and flown up in her.'

'Can they land here?' cried Paul.

'Of course!' said Mike. 'Look at this great smooth courtyard – an ideal landing-ground if ever there was one! Oh, if only Ranni and Pilescu know this mountain when they see it, and they come here!'

The aeroplane came nearer, rising high as it flew, as if it were going to fly right over the summit of the mountain. The Mountain Folk were terrified, and crouched to the ground. The aeroplane, gleaming as white as a gull, circled overhead as if it were looking for something.

'It's going to land, it's going to land!' yelled Jack, jumping about even though his hands and legs were bound. 'Golly, what a shock for the red-beards!'

The white aeroplane circled lower – and even as it made to land there came another noise echoing around the mountains.

'R-r-r-r-r-r! R-r-r-r-r-r!'

'That's *my* aeroplane; I bet it is, I bet it is!' yelled Prince Paul, his face red with excitement as he tried his hardest to get rid of the ropes that bound him, 'I'd know the sound of *my* aeroplane anywhere too!'

Whilst the White Swallow made a perfect landing, running gracefully on her big wheels over the enormous flat courtyard, the second aeroplane could be seen rising slowly up the mountainside.

'It's Paul's blue and silver plane,' cried Peggy. 'Oh, my goodness – this is too thrilling for anything! Look who's in the White Swallow! Ranni, Ranni, Ranni!'

A Thrilling Rescue!

The chief and his servants were full of amazement and fear when they heard the noise of the aeroplanes and saw them coming. When the White Swallow zoomed immediately overhead all the Mountain Folk fell down in fear and moaned as if they were in pain.

'Look out! You'll be hurt by the plane!' yelled Mike, when the White Swallow made to land. The terrified people leapt to their feet and ran helter-skelter to the sides of the courtyard. The plane missed everyone, and it was good to see Ranni's smiling face as he jumped down from the cockpit. He glanced at the Mountain Folk but none were near, and ran across the courtyard to the prisoners. He pulled a fierce-looking knife from his belt and cut them all free.

The children crowded round him, hugging him and raining questions. 'You should have seen me yesterday!' yelled Paul, who was now very proud of his narrow escape. 'I wore clothes of gold and sun-rays on my head!'

Captain and Mrs Arnold were delighted too, though the Captain kept a stern eye on the Mountain Folk, who were crowded together, trembling, watching the aeroplane.

'They look as if they expect it to jump on them, or bark at them or something,' grinned Jack.

'I think it would be a good thing if we took off at once,' said Ranni. 'You never know when these people will find their senses and start making things unpleasant for us! They've only got to damage our plane and we are done for!'

'Here comes Pilescu with *my* plane!' cried Paul in delight, as the big blue and silver aeroplane circled overhead, making a tremendous noise. The mountains around threw the echoes back, and the aeroplane sounded like a rumbling thunder-storm! Round and round it circled, and the Mountain Folk gave groans of terror and threw themselves on their faces again.

The little prince's plane made just as good a landing as the White Swallow. It let down its wheels and lightly touched the ground, running along smoothly over the

enormous courtyard.

'Really, it is a perfect landing-ground!' said Captain Arnold, watching. 'Smooth, big, and with plenty of wind!'

The blue and silver plane came to a stop. The door of the cockpit opened as the engines stopped. Pilescu looked out, his eyes hidden by sun-glasses. Ranni had not worn them, and the sight of Pilescu gave the Mountain Folk an even bigger fright!

Half of them rushed to the big stairway and disappeared down it, shouting. The other half, with the chief, knelt on the ground, the chief muttering something.

'He say, "Big chief want mercy!"' grinned Mafumu, who was now enjoying himself immensely.

'Well, if he thinks I'm going to throw him down the mountainside or take him off in the planes, he's mistaken,' said Captain Arnold. 'I shan't take any notice of him at all. Come along – we really ought to get off at once. It is a miraculous escape from great danger.'

'The two planes will easily take us all,' said Mike joyfully. 'Who's going in which?'

'Ranni, Pilescu, Paul, Jack and the girls can go in Paul's big plane,' said Captain Arnold. 'I'd like Mike with us – and Mafumu had better come with me too. We can't leave him here.'

They all began to climb up into the two cockpits. It didn't take long. Pilescu took the controls of his plane and looked round.

'All ready?' he asked. Then he looked again. 'Where's Paul? I thought he was to come in this plane.'

'He's not here,' said Jack. 'I expect he climbed into the White Swallow. I know he always wanted to fly in her.'

'Right,' said Pilescu, and pulled at a handle. But Ranni stopped him.

'We *must* see if Paul is in the other plane!' he said. 'We don't want to arrive in England and find that Paul isn't in either plane!'

Ranni opened the door of the cockpit again and leaned out. He yelled to the White Swallow. 'Hello there! Have you got Paul all right?'

'What?' yelled Captain Arnold, who was just about to take off.

'Is PAUL with you?' shouted Ranni.

'No,' shouted back Captain Arnold, after a quick look round his own plane. 'I said he was to go with you. The

White Swallow isn't big enough for more than four.'

Ranni went white. He loved the little Prince better than anyone else in the world – and here they were, about to take off from the mountain top without Paul! Whatever in the world had become of him?

Ranni leapt out of the plane. Nora called to him. 'Look. Isn't that Paul over there in the temple?'

Ranni rushed towards the temple, imagining that all kinds of dreadful things were happening to the little prince. He took out his gun, quite determined to give the whole of the Mountain Folk the worst shock of their lives if they were taking little Paul a prisoner again!

Nobody but Paul was in the temple. He was in a corner struggling with something. Ranni gave a roar.

'Paul! What is it? We nearly went without you!'

Paul stood up. In his arms was the beautiful shimmering robe of golden cloth that he had worn the day before, and over his shoulder he had slung his sun-ray headress. Young Paul was determined to take those back to school with him, to show his admiring friends. How else would they believe him when he told them of his great adventure?

He had slipped away from his party when no one was looking, for he had felt certain that Captain Arnold would say no, if he asked if he might go and get the garments. The clothes had been difficult to gather up and carry, and Paul did not realise that the planes were starting off so soon!

'Hello, Ranni! I just went to get these sun-clothes of mine,' said Paul. 'You haven't seen them, Ranni. Look, you must…'

177

But to Paul's enormous astonishment Ranni gave him a resounding slap, picked up the boy, clothes and all, and ran back to the big blue and silver plane with him. The Mountain Folk, seeing Ranni run, began to jabber, and one or two picked up their spears.

A gleaming spear flew past Ranni's big head. He dodged to one side, sprang up the ladder of the cockpit and threw Paul on to a seat.

'The little idiot had gone into the temple to get his sun-clothes!' said Ranni, angry and alarmed because they had so nearly gone without Paul.

Paul was angry too. He sat up on the seat. 'How dare you hit me?' he shouted to Ranni. 'I'll tell the King, my father. He'll, he'll, he'll…'

'Shut up, Paul,' said Jack. 'I'll hit you myself if you say any more! You might have stopped us escaping. The Mountain Folk are looking rather nasty now.'

Sure enough some of them were creeping towards the planes, spears in hand. Both planes started up their engines. The throbbing noise arose on the air again. The Mountain Folk shrank back in alarm.

The White Swallow took off first. Gracefully she rose into the air, circled round twice, and then made off over the mountains. Then the blue and silver plane rose up and she was off too.

Jack looked downwards. Already the Secret Mountain looked far off and small. He could just see the folk there running about like ants. How angry they must be because their prisoners had escaped in such an extraordinary way! 'Well, we're off again,' said Jack to the girls. 'And glad as I was to see the Secret Mountain,

I am even gladder to leave it behind! Cheer up, Paul, don't look so blue! We're safe now, even though you nearly messed things up!'

Prince Paul was feeling very foolish. 'Sorry,' he said. 'I didn't think. Anyway, thank goodness I've got the sun-clothes. Won't the boys at school think I'm lucky! I shall dress up in them and show the Head.'

Everyone laughed. It was exciting to be in the plane again. Jack called to Ranni.

'Ranni! You haven't told us your adventures yet. How did you escape from the Secret Mountain?'

'It was unexpectedly easy,' shouted back Ranni, who was sitting beside Pilescu. 'No one suspected that Pilescu and I were anything but ordinary Mountain Folk when we went down the golden stairway with them. We went down and down for ages and at last came to a big cave where most of them seem to live.'

'Oh yes, Mafumu and I once saw that,' said Jack. 'Go on, Ranni.'

'We didn't like to go and sit in the cave in case somebody spoke to us and we couldn't answer in their language,' said Ranni. 'So we waited about in a passage until we saw a little party of the Mountain Folk going along with spears. We thought they must be going hunting so we joined them, walking behind them.'

'How exciting!' said Nora. 'Didn't they guess who you were?'

'Not once,' said Ranni. 'We followed them down all kinds of dark passages until we came into the big hall-like place whose steps lead up to the rock-entrance. They worked a lever and the big door slid open. Then they set that great rock turning and sliding, and the way was open to us!'

'You *were* lucky,' said Jack. 'I wish I had shared that adventure.'

'It wasn't quite so good after that,' said Ranni. 'We had to find our way back to the planes and we got completely lost up in the mountain pass. We found our way at last by a great stroke of luck – and arrived at the planes, very tired indeed, but safe!'

'It didn't take you long to get them going,' shouted Peggy. 'Did you find it difficult to spot the Secret Mountain?'

'No. Very easy,' said Ranni. 'It looks so yellow from the air – and besides, it's the only one with a flat top.'

'I say! What's the White Swallow doing?' cried Jack suddenly. 'It's going down! Is it going to land, Ranni?'

'It looks like it,' said Ranni. 'I wonder what's the matter! My word, I hope nothing has gone wrong. This plane is large but it won't take everyone.'

The White Swallow flew lower still. Below was a fine flat stretch of grass, and the plane was making for that. It landed easily and came to a stop.

'We must land too, and see what's up,' said Ranni, looking worried. So the blue and silver plane circled round too, and flew slowly towards the flat piece of grass. It let down its wheels and landed gently and smoothly, running along for a little way and then stopping.

Captain Arnold was already out of his plane and was helping little Mafumu down.

'What's the matter? Anything wrong?' yelled Ranni, climbing from his cockpit. 'Let me come and help!'

Goodbye to Mafumu – and Home at Last!

Captain Arnold looked round and shook his head. 'No – there's nothing wrong,' he said. 'But we can't take Mafumu to England with us! He would be miserable away from his own people. His own folk live near here – look, you can see the village over there – and I am taking him home.'

'The children will want to say goodbye to him,' said Ranni at once. 'Little Mafumu has been a good friend to us. We couldn't have rescued you without his help. Hey, Jack – bring Paul and the girls to say goodbye to Mafumu. We're leaving him here.'

Everyone climbed from the two aeroplanes. The children were sad to say goodbye to their small friend. They had grown very fond of cheeky Mafumu, and they did not want to leave him behind at all.

'Can't we possibly take Mafumu home with us?' asked Paul. 'Do let's. He could live with us – and he could come to school with Mike and Jack and me!'

'Mafumu wouldn't be happy,' said Ranni. 'One day we will all pay a visit to him again, and see how he is getting on. I shouldn't be surprised if some day he is made chief of his tribe – he is brave and intelligent, and has all the makings of a fine leader.'

'I hope that uncle of his won't hit him too much,' said Jack. 'Golly, look – all the people are running out from the village. Have they seen Mafumu, do you think?'

Sure enough, from the little native village nearby came many men, women and children. They had seen Mafumu, and although they had been unsure about the aeroplanes, they felt that the 'big roaring birds' as they called them could not be very dangerous if Mafumu was in one of them!

Mafumu's uncle was with the people. Jack wondered if he would take hold of the little boy and give him a shaking for having run away from him back to his friends. He glanced at Mafumu to see if he was afraid. But the boy held himself proudly. Was he not friends with these people? Had he not helped them? He felt a real king that day.

'Mafumu, take this for a parting present,' said Prince Paul, and he gave Mafumu his best pocket-knife, a marvellous thing with a bright gold handle. Mafumu was overjoyed. He had often seen Paul using it, and had not even dared to ask if he might borrow it. Now it was his own! Mafumu could hardly believe his good luck.

And then, of course, everyone wanted to give little Mafumu something. Nora gave him a bead necklace, and Peggy gave him her little silver brooch with P on. Mafumu pinned it onto his shorts!

'P doesn't stand for Mafumu, but as he doesn't know his letters it doesn't matter,' said Peggy. 'What are you giving Mafumu, Mike?'

Mike had three fine glass marbles which he always carried about with him in his pocket. He gave them to Mafumu, whose eyes grew wider and wider as these presents were given to him! His teeth flashed white as he grinned round at everyone.

Jack gave him a pencil. It was a silver one, whose point went up or down when the bottom end was screwed round. Mafumu thought this was very clever and he was overjoyed to have the wonderful pencil for his own. He threw his arms round Jack and gave him a big hug.

'Stop it, Mafumu,' said Jack uncomfortably, for the others were giggling. But Mafumu hadn't finished, he hugged Jack again and again, so tightly that Jack nearly fell over.

'Shut up, Mafumu,' said Jack again. Mafumu at last let go. His eyes swimming in tears, for it nearly broke his little heart to part from Jack. He had nothing of his own to give Jack – except his very precious necklace of crocodile teeth! He took it off, muttered a few words over it, and then pressed it into Jack's hand.

'No, Mafumu,' said Jack. 'No. I know quite well that you think these crocodile teeth are your special good luck charm and keep you from danger. I don't want them.'

But Mafumu would not take no for an answer, and in the end Jack put the crocodile necklace into his pocket, feeling a funny lump in his throat. Dear old Mafumu – it wasn't easy to part from him.

Ranni gave the boy a little mirror for himself. Pilescu gave him a notebook to scribble in with his new pencil. Captain Arnold gave him an old pair of sunglasses, which were in a locker at the back of the White Swallow. These nearly sent Mafumu mad with joy. He at once put them on, and looked so peculiar that everyone shrieked with laughter.

And then Mrs Arnold gave the boy a photograph of all the children. It was one that she always took about with her, and was in a brown leather folding frame. Mafumu was so pleased that he did a kind of war-dance, holding all his gifts above his head, and wearing his sunglasses over his eyes. Everyone laughed till their sides ached.

The folk from the village had come nearer and nearer, full of amazement to see Mafumu receiving gifts from his friends. Mafumu took off his sunglasses and beamed round at the children.

'Goodbye,' he said, in English. 'Goodbye. Come again. Mafumu is your friend.'

Everyone hugged Mafumu and then they got back into the planes. The villagers came right up to Mafumu when they saw that the others were safely in the 'big roaring birds.' Mafumu's uncle was jealous. He wanted the necklace that Nora had given to little Mafumu. The boy glared at his uncle. Then, with a quick movement, he put on his sunglasses and shouted in a most warlike manner.

With shrieks the whole of the villagers ran away, Mafumu's uncle running the fastest. Then Mafumu, with slow and stately steps, stalked after them, feeling himself a very chief of chiefs! That was the last sight the children had of their small friend, for the two planes took off. Mafumu turned for a moment and waved. Then, too proud to feel sad just then, he went on his way to his village, feeling quite certain that his cruel uncle would not try many more tricks on him!

'I do hate leaving Mafumu behind,' sighed Peggy. 'I really do hate it. He's quite one of us.'

'Jack's lucky to have those crocodile teeth,' said Paul.

'And you're lucky to have that glorious, shimmering robe and sun-ray head-dress,' said Peggy. 'I wish I had it!'

'I'll lend it to you whenever you want it,' said Paul generously. 'I truly will.'

The aeroplanes were flying well and fast. Nora looked down to see if they were still over mountains and she gave a cry.

'We're over the Secret Mountain again! Look, everybody! We must have gone out of our way to take Mafumu back – and now we're flying the opposite way home.'

Everyone looked down. Yes – there was the Secret Mountain, with its curious yellow colouring. And there was the flat top, with the vast smooth courtyard on which had happened their most exciting adventures.

'Wasn't the eclipse fun?' said Nora.

'And didn't Paul look marvellous when he came up that stairway dressed in those wonderful robes?' said Peggy.

'And wasn't it glorious when we stood on the top of

the mountain and suddenly heard the roar of the White Swallow's engines?' said Jack.

'I wish we could have this adventure all over again,' said Paul. 'It was a bit too exciting at times, but I like exciting things.'

'Well, let's hope the adventure is finished as far as excitement and danger are concerned,' said Ranni. 'I've had quite enough, I can tell you! All I want now is to get back to England safely, and see you all safe and sound at school again!'

'School! Fancy going back to school after all this!' cried Paul. 'I don't want to. I want to go off flying in my plane again, Ranni.'

'You can want all you like, but school is the best and safest place for *you*,' said Ranni. 'And, anyway, you have plenty to tell the boys. My word, they'll think you a hero, you may be sure!'

'Will they really?' asked the little prince, his eyes shining. 'I'm not really a hero – but I wouldn't a bit mind people thinking me one.'

The planes flew on steadily. At last they came to a big airport, where they landed. They took in fuel and the children had a good meal. Captain Arnold sent a message to England to say that they were all safe and sound. Then off they set again.

The children slept the night through peacefully. Adventures were lovely – but it *was* nice to feel safe again. They began to look forward to seeing England and Dimmy, and to telling their tremendous story.

And at last they were home! They landed at the big airport, and what a crowd was there to welcome them!

Photographers ran up to take their picture, people crowded up to clap them on the backs and to shake hands, and Captain Arnold had to speak a few words into a microphone to say they were safely back at last!

Then they all squeezed into two cars and off they went to London and to Dimmy. They chattered and laughed, excited and proud. It was grand to be back home again, and to be welcomed in such a lovely way.

Dimmy was standing on the steps to welcome them herself. The children tumbled out of the cars and rushed to her, shouting their news.

'We've been to Africa!'

'We found a Secret Mountain!'

'Paul was nearly made a sacrifice to the sun!'

'An eclipse came, and the people thought we had killed the sun!'

'Well, you'll certainly kill *me* if you hug me like this!' said Dimmy, her eyes full of happy tears, because she was so thankful to see them again. She had been terribly worried and anxious when all the children had left her so suddenly – but now everything was all right!

That evening Captain Arnold had to go off to broadcast his story. It was to be at a quarter past nine, after the news. The children switched on the radio and listened in. It was fun to hear Captain Arnold's deep voice booming into the room as he began the tale of their adventures.

Dimmy listened in amazement. She had already heard bits and pieces from the children, but here was the tale told in full, just as it might be written in a book. It was marvellous!

For half an hour the tale went on – and then it was over. Dimmy switched off the radio.

'Well, well,' she said, 'we've been through some adventures together, children – but this one is the most exciting of all. Did it really happen? Could such things happen to ordinary children like you?'

'Well, they *did*!' said Jack, and he showed Dimmy his necklace of crocodile teeth. 'Look here – these are teeth from a crocodile that nearly ate Mafumu one day. His father and uncles killed it, and gave Mafumu some of the teeth. And he gave them to me.'

'I wonder what Mafumu is doing now,' said Mike. 'Wasn't he a fine friend? We wouldn't be here now if it wasn't for Mafumu.'

'And you're not going to be *here* much longer,' said Dimmy, getting up. 'It's long past your bedtime!'

'*Bed*time! Is there such a thing as *bed*time?' said Peggy. 'I'd forgotten all about it! We haven't been properly to bed for weeks. I don't think I shall really bother about bedtime any more.'

'Well, *you* may not – but I shall!' said Dimmy. 'Come along, all of you. *Bedtime*! There are biscuits and lemonade for those who come now – and none for those who dawdle!'

So biscuits and lemonade it was, and a long, long talk in the bedrooms! And then Dimmy firmly switched off the lights, tucked everybody up, said, 'No more talking,' in a very stern voice – and left them.

We must leave them, too, dreaming of their adventures – dreaming of the strange, far-away Secret Mountain!